MONTANA MAVERICKS

Welcome to Big Sky Country, home of the Montana Mavericks! Where free-spirited men and women discover love on the range.

THE ANNIVERSARY GIFT

The mayor of Bronco and his wife have invited the whole town to help celebrate their thirtieth anniversary, but when the pearl necklace the mayor bought his wife goes missing at the party, it sets off a chain of events that brings together some of Bronco's most unexpected couples. Call it coincidence, call it fate—or call it what it is: the power of true love to win over the hardest cowboy hearts!

For the past two years, widowed rodeo rider Elizabeth Hawkins has been raising her twin daughters alone, far from family and friends. Rancher Jake McCreery, a widowed father of three, understands in a way few others can. With Elizabeth planning to return to Australia soon, Jake knows he should keep his distance. Yet he can't help picturing them as a couple—of the permanent kind...

Dear Reader,

Love has returned to Bronco, Montana. This time it has set its sights on Elizabeth Hawkins and Jake McCreery.

Elizabeth is a widowed single mother of five-year-old twins. She is at a crossroads, trying to decide whether to move to America to be closer to her family, or go back home to Australia and everything that is familiar to her daughters. The last thing she needs is a man complicating her life and making this decision more difficult.

Jake is a widower with three kids of his own. He is doing his best to raise his kids, although lately, he's had difficulty connecting with his tween daughter. His plate is full and there isn't room for anyone else in his life.

The kids take an instant liking to each other, so although Elizabeth and Jake are not looking for romance, they are open to friendship. Their kids have other ideas. With five little matchmakers determined to become a family, will Jake and Elizabeth take a chance on loving again?

I hope you enjoy reading *Starting Over with the Maverick* as much as I enjoyed writing it.

I love hearing from my readers, so feel free to visit my website, kathydouglassbooks.com, and drop me a line.

Happy reading!

Kathy

STARTING OVER WITH THE MAVERICK

KATHY DOUGLASS

HARLEQUIN

Special thanks and acknowledgment are given to
Kathy Douglass for her contribution to
the Montana Mavericks: The Anniversary Gift miniseries.

ISBN-13: 978-1-335-59478-5

Starting Over with the Maverick

Harlequin Enterprises ULC
22 Adelaide St. West, 41st Floor
Toronto, Ontario M5H 4E3, Canada
www.Harlequin.com

Printed in Lithuania

Recycling programs for this product may not exist in your area.

MIX
Paper | Supporting responsible forestry
FSC® C021394

Kathy Douglass is a lawyer turned author of sweet small-town contemporary romances. She is married to her very own hero and mother to two sons, who cheer her on as she tries to get her stubborn hero and heroine to realize they are meant to be together. She loves hearing from readers that something in her books made them laugh or cry. You can learn more about Kathy or contact her at kathydouglassbooks.com.

Books by Kathy Douglass

Montana Mavericks: The Anniversary Gift

Starting Over with the Maverick

Harlequin Special Edition

Montana Mavericks: Lassoing Love

Falling for Dr. Maverick

Aspen Creek Bachelors

Valentines for the Rancher
The Rancher's Baby
Wrangling a Family

Montana Mavericks: Brothers & Broncos

In the Ring with the Maverick

The Fortunes of Texas: The Wedding Gift

A Fortune in the Family

Furever Yours

The City Girl's Homecoming

Montana Mavericks: What Happened to Beatrix?

The Maverick's Baby Arrangement

Visit the Author Profile page
at Harlequin.com for more titles.

This book is dedicated with much love to my husband and sons. I appreciate your constant support.

This book is also dedicated to my parents, who instilled the love of reading in me at a very young age. I miss you both every day.

Chapter One

Elizabeth Hawkins walked into the arena of the Bronco Convention Center and looked around. Although it was located in Bronco, Montana, half a world from the ones she'd spent her time working in back in Queensland, Australia, the surroundings felt familiar, and she was immediately at ease. As a member of the famed rodeo Hawkins family, she had spent most of her adult life traveling the rodeo circuit. Unlike her cousins who performed in the United States and three of her sisters who toured in South America, Elizabeth and her sister Carly were based in Australia. Her sisters Tori, Amy, and Faith had moved to Bronco and had urged Elizabeth to join them.

Tori had visited Elizabeth and her daughters in Australia last year. They'd had so much fun just being together, and Elizabeth had realized how much she'd missed having her family around. Now that her girls were approaching school age, she was faced with a decision. Should she move to the United States, where several of her sisters and her extended family lived, or should she stay in Australia and attempt to live the life she and her late husband, Arlo, had planned? The life they'd dreamed of? She didn't know, which was why she and her daughters were staying in Tori's old cabin on the outskirts of Bronco on an extended vacation—now that Tori had moved in with her fiancé, Bobby Stone. She needed facts in order to make an informed decision.

"What do you think?" Rylee Parker asked, bringing Elizabeth's attention to the present and the reason they were meeting today. Rylee was the marketing director of the Bronco Convention Center, and she'd been showing Elizabeth around.

"It's nice. The perfect venue to host a rodeo."

"Not just rodeos—although those are popular," Rylee said. "We're the preferred venue for everything from sales conventions to classic-car shows. What we're interested in hosting is something rodeo-related with you."

"Of course." It made good business sense for Rylee to capitalize on the Hawkins name. Her cousins—Brynn, Audrey, Remi, and Corinne—were big celebrities in the American rodeo world and lived in Bronco when not touring. Audrey, easily the best competitor on the woman's circuit, had recently married Jack Burris, one of the uberfamous rodeo Burris brothers who'd grown up in Bronco. The Hawkins Sisters had even competed against the Burris brothers in a Battle of the Sexes a couple of years back, an event that had given them and women's rodeo a higher profile in the United States. "What did you have in mind?"

"I have a couple of ideas, but I hoped we could brainstorm and come up with something new and fresh."

Before Elizabeth could respond, one of her daughters patted her thigh. Squelching a sigh, she looked down at Gianna, the older of her five-year-old twins by two minutes. Lucy and Gianna had once been so outgoing and confident, much like their charming father. Arlo, Elizabeth's beloved husband, had never met a stranger. Also like their father, Lucy and Gianna had been daredevils, willing to try anything. Elizabeth had found her heart in her throat on more than one occasion as she'd watched her little girls try to match the skills performed by older kids on the rodeo circuit. Arlo had always laughed and assured her that their girls could do anything. More than that, he'd always stood nearby, ready to catch them if they should fall. Gianna and Lucy were gifted athletes, and it was rare that Arlo had needed to save them. But his presence had been enough to allay all of Elizabeth's fears.

Sadly Arlo had succumbed to an unexpected heart attack two years ago and was no longer around to protect their little family or calm Elizabeth's fears.

Elizabeth swallowed hard, forcing away the unhappy memory. Although she had gotten over the agony that had accompanied his death, the occasional pang struck her at unexpected and inopportune times. Over the years, she'd learned to work through the pain, pasting on a smile and soldiering on. She was responsible for her daughters and didn't have the luxury of indulging her feelings. Her daughters had lost their father to a hidden health defect. They couldn't afford to lose their mother to grief. So no matter how desperately she'd longed to curl up into a ball and cry, she'd forced herself to carry on. *Fake it until you make it* had become her mantra.

"Are we done yet?" Gianna whispered.

Lucy moved closer to her sister. The two of them had become quiet after Arlo's death. Over time, with the love of their paternal grandparents and rodeo family, they'd begun to become the little girls they had been. Since they'd been in the States, the girls had begun to cling again.

"Not quite," Elizabeth replied. She'd wanted to leave the girls with one of her sisters or cousins while she met with Rylee, but the girls had kicked up a fuss. They weren't ready to let her out of their sight. Not that she blamed them.

They were in an unfamiliar environment. Although people here spoke the same language for the most part, they did so with an accent, emphasizing just how far away from home they were.

"How much longer are we going to be here?" Lucy asked, her voice pitched even lower than her sister's.

"Not much longer. Do you girls want to sit on the benches and play with your dolls?"

Gianna and Lucy glanced over at the risers on the far side of the arena and then shook their heads.

Elizabeth flashed Rylee an apologetic smile. "Sorry."

"Don't be. I understand," she said. "I imagine they're still trying to get used to their new surroundings."

"Yes." Elizabeth stepped between her daughters, put her arms around their shoulders and gave them each a gentle hug. There had been so many changes in their young lives, requiring them to get their bearings over and over. Now they were in a strange country with a whole host of new relatives who kept coming around, wanting to spend time with them. Was it any wonder they were glued to her side? She was the only bit of familiarity they had. "If you want to reschedule our meeting to a later date, I'm willing."

Rylee waved her hand. "There's no need for that. I love kids. In fact, I often babysit my neighbor's toddler, so I can imagine how they're feeling right now. Your daughters are sweeties."

"Thanks for understanding. This isn't the usual way I conduct business."

"Since we're putting on a program for kids, it will be good to get their opinion. They can be our consultants." She stooped down and spoke directly to the girls. "Would you like to be our helpers?"

The girls grinned and looked up at Elizabeth.

Gianna gave a tentative smile. "Can we?"

"Absolutely," she said.

Gianna and Lucy nodded at Rylee. "Okay."

Elizabeth smiled. It was nice to know that Rylee understood her situation as a single mother of two young children. Although this was her first time meeting Rylee, she liked the other woman and believed they could become friends. "I appreciate that. But will it be okay with your boss? I don't want to cause any problems for you."

"Not at all. We have actually been talking about starting an on-site day care for employees. I don't know if you're interested, but there are a couple of day cares in town you might want to check out."

"My daughters have never been in day care. When my late husband or I weren't able to care for them, our friends on the tour looked out for them. When we were home, my in-laws were there with open arms."

"I'm sure that was wonderful."

"It was." If she moved here, she would lose that connection and those relationships. "So what did you have in mind for programming?"

"We were thinking about horse-riding camp. While there are plenty of ranches surrounding Bronco, lots of children in town don't have access to horses. Plenty of kids here have not even seen a horse close up. They don't know how to ride or care for them."

That statement was disappointing, especially given how many ranches were nearby. Elizabeth would do whatever she could to help remedy the situation. "My girls have been riding since they were two. They love being on horseback. This program sounds like something that would benefit a lot of kids. How would we make it work?"

"So you're on board?" Rylee flashed a hopeful smile.

"Yes. A pony academy sounds like it's needed in this town. But I'm not sure how long I'll be in Bronco. I don't want to make a commitment that I can't keep. It would be wrong to get the kids excited only to disappoint them."

"How about we start with a day and limit it to kids ten and under?" Rylee said. "They can't be disappointed if they only expect one day."

"That's true. I can definitely commit to a day. If there's a lot of interest, I'm open to having a second day."

"That sounds good. Now we just need to come up with a catchy name."

"I suggest we keep it simple. Kids like to belong to clubs, so how about we call it the Pony Club?"

Rylee nodded. "That works for me. And it sums up exactly what the event will be about."

They firmed up the details and finished the tour of the convention center.

"I look forward to working with you," Rylee said when they were standing by the entrance.

"Same," Elizabeth said honestly. She took her girls by the hand and led them to the parking lot. Once they were in the car she inhaled deeply. She wasn't sure what the future held, but she'd taken a small step by agreeing to lead the Pony Club. She hoped Arlo would approve.

"Come on—hurry up so we won't be late." Molly picked up a boot and handed it to her brother, standing over him until he put it on.

"I don't need you watching," Pete said, shoving in his foot. He turned to look at his dad, who had been helping Ben to get ready. "Dad, tell Molly to stop bossing me around."

Jake McCreery blew out a sigh and looked at his two oldest children. At ten years old, Molly often acted as a mother hen. Generally Pete, two years younger, didn't mind her hovering. But today he was annoyed. At times like this, Jake missed his late wife Maggie's calm guiding hand. Although she'd died six years ago, giving birth to Ben, Jake still wondered how she would handle these dustups. *WWMD—What would Maggie do?*—had become his go-to phrase when things got rough. No doubt she would have the perfect solution that left everyone happy. But since she was gone, it was up to him to handle the situation.

"Molly, your brother is capable of getting ready on his own. Perhaps you should make sure you have everything you need."

Molly gave Pete one last exasperated look and then looked at Jake. "I just want to be on time to the Pony Club."

"I understand."

"All of our friends are going to be there."

Jake nodded. Even though they had plenty of horses of their own, he'd signed up his kids for the Pony Club. It would be good for his brood to be around other kids. Especially Molly. She often gravitated toward activities geared for older people where she would be surrounded by mother figures. Case in point, she'd been the youngest contestant in the Valentine's Day bakeoff at Bronco Motors earlier this year. Jake had been proud of her, of course, but he wanted her to spend time with other kids. She tended to act more her age around the girls in her class.

"Yeah," Pete agreed, his temporary pique with his sister a thing of the past. But then, Pete was too good-natured to hold a grudge. "Plus real rodeo stars are going to be there. With their winning belt buckles."

"And their horses," Ben piped up. He grinned, showing off the hole where his right front tooth used to be.

"Well, then, let's hit the road," Jake said.

Once everyone was loaded into the SUV, he headed toward the Bronco Convention Center.

Bronco, Montana, was two towns in one: the ritzy Bronco Heights and the middle-class Bronco Valley. Although there were differences—the obvious ones being the wealth disparity—for the most part the citizens got along well. Jake's ranch was about forty-five minutes outside town, so he didn't make it here on a regular basis. But when he did, he enjoyed treating himself and his kids to ribs at DJ's Deluxe or shakes at Bronco Burgers.

The kids chattered happily about the club and what they hoped would happen. From the sound of it, they had extremely high expectations. Jake crossed his fingers that they wouldn't be disappointed.

When they arrived, Jake parked and then stood back while the kids jumped from the vehicle. After Maggie's death, Jake had become very protective of his kids, afraid to lose another person that he loved. Disaster had struck once, taking his beloved wife without warning. For a while, Jake had seen the potential for disaster around every corner, waiting to pounce on one of his children.

Ben was the third child, so by that time Jake should have had the father thing down to a science. He'd experienced the bumps and bruises, the fevers and crying jags twice before. Even knowing what to expect, he'd been a bundle of nerves with Ben, blowing every little thing out of proportion.

Luckily, the past six years had been uneventful. There had been no disasters, and over time, he'd begun to relax and had stopped expecting the worst to happen. Now a bump on the head was simply a bump on the head and not a potential concussion that required a trip to the doctor.

At the same time, his grief had faded. Even so, he still missed Maggie and always would. She'd been the best part of his life. He hated that she'd been cheated out of the opportunity to watch her children grow up. Knowing that she wouldn't be there for birthdays and graduations broke his heart. But he couldn't wallow in grief. Not when he had three children depending on him.

There were several cars and trucks parked in the lot—a clear sign that the Pony Club was going to be popular with the kids in town. Two kids who lived on a nearby ranch hopped out of an SUV and ran into the convention center. Apparently his three weren't the only ranch kids attending the club today.

Jake and his kids stepped inside. The sound of horses neighing filled the air. Without saying a word, the kids took off running. Not wanting to let them get too far ahead of him, he jogged behind them. When he reached the floor of the arena, he noticed several things at once. First, there were several kids—including Ben and Pete—clustered around rodeo star Ross Burris and talking a mile a minute as they pointed at the horses. Second, his daughter wasn't with them.

He looked around until he spotted her. She was talking to two little girls dressed in rodeo garb and paying no attention to the animals. Given that they had horses at home, that wasn't completely unexpected. Even so, he felt a twinge of guilt. It couldn't be easy for her to be the only female in the house. He tried to get in touch with his feminine side—whatever the heck that meant—but he knew he could never take the place of her mother. There hadn't been anyone to give her female guidance for six years.

Not that there weren't women eager to step into that role. Women had been trying to become a part of his family for years. Maggie had only been gone two weeks before they'd begun circling. Of all the things that had hurt and disappointed him, that had been the worst. He couldn't believe women who had known his wife for years, women who had been her friends, had suddenly thought that they could take her place in her family. *In his heart*. He hadn't looked at any of them the same way since.

Jake blew out a long breath, hoping to expel the negativity. Since his boys were in good hands, Jake made his way over to Molly. She smiled and waved excitedly at him.

"This is Lucy and Gianna," she said when he was standing in front of her. "They're identical twins."

He didn't recognize them. Perhaps they were new to town.

"Hello, Lucy. Hello, Gianna." He glanced at each girl as he spoke, hoping that he'd addressed them correctly.

The girls giggled, leaving him unsure if he'd gotten their names right. Although they were wearing rodeo costumes, their outfits were different colors. If he could get the names straight now, he would know which girl was wearing purple and which girl was wearing blue.

"They don't talk like us," Molly said, sounding amazed and impressed. "They have accents."

"Is that right?" he asked, looking from one girl to the next. They only stared at him. Then they moved closer together. The movement was nearly imperceptible, but he noticed it. He took a step away from them. The last thing he wanted was to make them uncomfortable.

"But to them, you're the one with the accent."

Jake turned at the sound of a woman's slightly accented voice. He took one look at her and gasped. Women were often described as *breathtaking*, although he'd never used that word before today. It fit her perfectly. She'd literally taken his breath away.

The woman was dressed in rodeo garb too. The fitted jeans emphasized her slender legs and curvy hips. Her fringed blouse floated over perky breasts and tapered down to her small waist.

He could listen to her sultry voice for days, but if he wanted the conversation to continue, he had to speak. Holding out a hand, he smiled. "I'm Jake McCreery. Molly's father."

"It's nice to meet you, Jake McCreery," the woman replied, taking the hand he offered. "I'm Elizabeth Hawkins."

Her brown skin was soft, and he felt the strangest tingling at the contact. It had been some time since he'd reacted physically toward a woman. He'd thought that part of him had died with Maggie. Over the past six years, nothing had changed that belief. At the urging of friends, he'd gone on the occasional date. Nothing had ever come of them. He'd laughed at jokes, had a drink or shared a meal, and had come home to his empty bed—never feeling a hint of the attraction he'd felt when he'd met Maggie. But maybe they had been the wrong person, because all of a sudden, his body was letting him know it was still in the game.

He checked her left hand and didn't see a ring. "Hawkins? That's a popular name in rodeo. Especially here in Bronco. Are you related to the Hawkins Sisters?"

She nodded, and her lovely hair brushed her shoulders. It was wavy, and his fingers ached to see if it was as soft as it looked. "Actually I'm one of them. My sisters just moved to Bronco after touring South America. And there's also my cousins."

"From the sound of it, rodeo is in your blood."

She laughed. "I don't know if you can say that."

"Your cousins and sisters are in rodeo. As are you. What more proof do I need?"

"You can say it runs in the family, but not so much in the blood."

"I don't see the difference."

"My sisters and I and many of my cousins are adopted. We're the same family, but we don't share blood."

"It's the love that makes a family," he said. "Not the genetics."

"I couldn't have said it better." Her bright smile touched his heart, and he smiled in return.

"Mummy, when are we going to start the club?"

Elizabeth checked her watch and then tapped the little girl on the nose. "In ten minutes, Gianna. Are you both ready?"

Ah, so Gianna was dressed in blue. That meant that Lucy was wearing purple. He'd gotten it wrong before. Jake made a mental note so he wouldn't make that mistake a second time.

"Ready," Gianna said.

"Ready," Lucy echoed, giving a little jump to emphasize the word.

"Do you need help?" Jake didn't know where that question came from. He was strictly here as a parent. Besides, he was sure the organizers had everything under control.

Elizabeth shook her head. "That's very kind of you to offer, but we've got it handled. Ross Burris and I will talk to the kids about life in the rodeo. After that we'll show the kids how to get on the horses and guide them on a quick trip around the arena. Finally we'll show them how to care for the animals."

"That sounds like a good plan. I'm sure the town kids will enjoy the new experience."

She tilted her head. Though there was nothing special about the move, she looked even more attractive. "I get the feeling that Molly isn't one of them."

"Nah. I live on a ranch outside town. We have horses, but my kids—Molly, Pete, and Ben—wanted to come."

She nodded. "There's something special about being around horses, even if you have one of your own."

"Plus there's the opportunity to meet rodeo stars."

She laughed. "That might apply to Ross Burris, but I live in Australia, so I'm sure none of the kids know who I am. Which is fine with me."

"Oh, so that's where your accent comes from. It's subtle—definitely not as pronounced as your daughters'—but it's there."

"I was born and raised in the States, but I moved to Australia about a decade ago. Over time I guess I picked up an accent."

"How long will you be in town?"

"I'm not sure. Definitely a few weeks more. This is an extended vacation to reconnect with my family. My sister lives with her fiancé, so she's letting us stay in her cabin. It's much better than a hotel."

Elizabeth's answer disappointed him, although he couldn't put his finger on why. He'd just met her, so why did he want her to stay around longer? The answer came immediately. He hadn't experienced anything remotely like the intense attraction he felt for Elizabeth with any of his dates. But then, perhaps her leaving was for the best. That way he didn't have to worry about this attraction turning into something that could result in pain. He'd had enough of that to last a lifetime.

"I hope you have a nice visit."

"So far my daughters and I are enjoying ourselves. It's been wonderful to see my family again."

"I bet. Thanks for letting my daughter hang out with your little girls. Molly is the only girl in the family. I think that she gets tired of just her brothers for company." He didn't know why he'd divulged that, especially to a stranger, but there was something about Elizabeth that encouraged sharing confidences.

"Molly is a sweet girl." She checked her watch and sighed. "It's time for me to get the event started. I need to corral my girls. They really enjoyed spending time with Molly."

"She was happy to do it. She's a little mother hen, so having two little girls around is right up her alley. But now I'll nab her and we'll join my boys." He gestured to Molly and then turned back to Elizabeth. "It was nice meeting you."

"It was nice meeting you too."

After Molly said so long to the twins, Jake steered her over to the boys. Pete and Ben were part of the group still gathered around Ross Burris. Ross had been born and raised in Bronco and was one of the famous Burris brothers. Although he wasn't as big a star as his brothers, Geoff and Jack, he'd done his share of winning on the rodeo circuit.

Ross told the kids to grab seats so they could get started.

Molly sat by her brothers, and Jake stood in the back, near enough to hear the presentation but far enough away not to be a distraction. Now that they were getting older, Molly and Pete liked to be on their own. They didn't want him hovering and watching their every move, so he tried to be as inconspicuous as possible. Besides, he wanted them to feel confident.

Thoughts of Elizabeth filled his mind, and he glanced in her direction. She was talking to a group of younger kids, holding the reins of her horse and allowing them to rub the animal's side. Her little girls were near her, showing off their costumes to a couple of other little girls who were duly impressed.

Jake couldn't seem to drag his eyes away from her. Just looking at her made his blood surge through his veins. With intelligent brown eyes, high cheekbones, and full kissable lips, she was truly beautiful.

"Any questions?" Ross Burris asked, pulling Jake's attention away from Elizabeth.

A little girl raised her hand. When Ross pointed at her, she asked her question. "Are you married?"

He smiled, unbothered by the query, although Jake was sure it was not along the line he'd intended. Ross glanced over at an attractive woman sitting in the bleachers, taking notes. "As a matter of fact, I am. That's my wife, Celeste, right there."

The little girl nodded slowly. "Oh."

"My daddy isn't married," Ben added, unprompted. "My mommy died a long time ago. Daddy is never going to get married again. Me and Pete and Molly don't need a mom. We're fine just the way we are. Us four and no more."

Jake's heart sank as his son confidently parroted the words he'd heard all of his life. When Pete and Molly nodded in agreement, Jake wondered if he'd done the wrong thing by insisting they were fine on their own. In trying to protect himself and his children from pain, had he made a mistake by telling them repeatedly they didn't need anyone else?

If so, how could he remedy that?

Chapter Two

"We're ready to go to the Pony Club, Mummy," Gianna said bright and early the next morning. It had taken the girls a couple of days to adjust to the sixteen-hour time difference, but once they had gotten used to being in American Mountain Daylight Time, they once more began waking up at the crack of dawn. It had taken Elizabeth a bit longer to adapt, but she was in the swing of things now too.

She and Arlo used to wake up early in order to enjoy quiet moments together, watching the sunrise and sipping coffee before starting their busy days. Elizabeth had tried to maintain that tradition after Arlo's death, but the dawn was too quiet. Too lonely. Now she only awoke with enough time to shower and dress before the girls began to stir.

Elizabeth set two bowls onto the small kitchen table before turning to look at her daughters. They were dressed similarly to the way they'd been yesterday, only this time in pink and green outfits. She'd left out short sets for them, but obviously they'd ignored them.

"Is that right?" she asked.

"Yes." Gianna and Lucy pulled out chairs and sat down.

Elizabeth set plates of Vegemite toast beside their bowls of Weet-Bix to round off their breakfast. She'd brought along some of their favorite foods for their vacation and was glad she had. Faith had cooked a typical American breakfast for them one day, and the girls hadn't been pleased at all. They'd taken one look at the plate of grits and bacon and turned up their noses. Since she remembered how strange some Australian foods had seemed to her when she'd first moved there, Elizabeth understood. If she and the girls decided to make a home in America, Elizabeth would do her best to help them adjust. Luckily, her friends and her sister Carly were willing to ship cases of their favorites to make the transition less painful.

"I told you that the club was only for one day. Remember?"

"But we want to go back. We want to play with Molly again," Gianna said.

"We like Molly," Lucy added before she took a big bite of her toast.

"I like Molly too," Elizabeth said, "but she's not at the convention center today since there is no Pony Club."

"Then where is she?" Gianna asked.

"I imagine that she's at home at this time of day," Elizabeth said.

"Then ring her and tell her we want to play again," Lucy said as if it was the most natural thing in the world. And to her, it was. They'd grown up in a close-knit rodeo community where getting together to play with their friends was simple.

Now that they'd made a new pal, Elizabeth wanted to nurture that friendship. She was willing to do whatever it took to help her daughters feel at home in Bronco for however long they stayed.

Elizabeth thought of the list of names, addresses, and phone numbers on the registration forms for the Pony Club. Jake McCreery's phone number would be in that file. Of course, it had been for camp use, not her personal use. Would it be crossing the line to call him to schedule a playdate?

Just thinking about Jake brought his image to her mind, and her heart skipped a beat as she recalled how attractive he was. He was about six feet, solidly built with ruddy skin, dark hair and expressive brown eyes. Dressed in well-worn jeans and a tan T-shirt that had clung to his broad shoulders, he'd stirred up longings in her that had lain dormant for two years. She hadn't been attracted to a man other than Arlo since she'd first laid eyes on him nine years ago. One look was all it had taken to fall madly in love. Now she was experiencing a similar attraction to Jake. She wasn't comfortable with the reaction, but she knew that it was easier to talk about controlling your feelings than it was to do it.

She'd enjoyed chatting with Jake and wished their conversation could have gone on longer, but she'd had a job to do. Perhaps that had been for the best. Her life was in flux. She was struggling to figure out her next move for her little family, so she didn't need to add another person to the mix. Besides, she didn't know whether she would even be in the United States two months from now, so it would be ridiculous to start something she wouldn't be able to finish.

She shook her head, trying to dislodge that foolish notion. Who said anything about starting a relationship? They'd only talked for fifteen minutes. Nowhere near enough time to get to know someone. Not only that, he'd given no indication that he was interested in anything other than killing time. He certainly hadn't done anything to make her believe that he was attracted to her.

"Why not?" Gianna asked.

"Why not what?"

"You shook your head? Why can't we ring Molly?"

Elizabeth bit back a laugh. That was what happened when you had conversations with yourself. "I think we can ring her. But not until later. She might still be sleeping. Let's finish our breakfast first."

"Then you'll ring her?" Lucy said. Gianna might've been the spokesperson for the two, but Lucy always sought confirmation. Elizabeth had no doubt that her younger daughter would be demanding things in writing once she could read better.

"Yes."

Satisfied with Elizabeth's reply, the girls talked to each other as they ate. As someone who'd grown up close to her own sisters, Elizabeth was pleased that her daughters were good friends.

Gianna's and Lucy's lives mirrored Elizabeth's and her sisters' childhood in so many ways. Elizabeth and her sisters were third-generation rodeo performers. They'd been raised on the circuit in much the same way that Elizabeth was raising Gianna and Lucy.

Though they'd emailed, texted, and FaceTimed each other regularly, Elizabeth hadn't realized just how much she'd missed her family until Tori's visit. When they'd embraced, Elizabeth had broken down in uncharacteristic tears. Tori had been crying too. Tori had wanted Elizabeth to commit to moving back to the States, but Elizabeth could only promise to come for an extended visit. Tori's cabin wasn't the biggest, but it was cozy. Besides, she and the girls enjoyed each other's company and didn't need much space.

The girls finished their breakfast and then showed their empty dishes to Elizabeth before putting them into the sink.

"Good job," she said. "You're such good helpers."

The girls smiled, and then Gianna asked, "Are you going to ring Molly's daddy now?"

"Yes." Elizabeth found Jake's number and grabbed her phone. Since it was such a nice day, she went outside and sat on the porch step. After grabbing their dolls, the girls followed. They jumped into the white wicker rocking chairs, waiting for her to make the call.

Elizabeth dialed his number and then listened as the phone rang. Her heartbeat sped up as she waited for him to answer. Telling herself not to be ridiculous, she inhaled deeply so she wouldn't sound like a breathless teenager.

Jake answered on the third ring, and his baritone "Hello?" sent shivers down Elizabeth's spine.

Determined to ignore her body's reaction, she echoed his greeting before continuing, "This is Elizabeth Hawkins. I hope I didn't wake you."

His laughter was filled with mirth. "You're kidding, right? I have three kids. Getting them up during the school year may be next to impossible, but I don't have that problem in the summer. They're up with the sun."

"I wonder what the difference is," she said dryly.

"Oh, I think you can guess. Not to mention that I'm a rancher. Although I have a foreman who helps a lot with supervising the ranch hands, we meet most mornings to go over plans for the day."

"I got your phone number from the permission slip you signed when you registered your kids for the Pony Club. I hope it's okay that I used it."

"It is."

"Great. Please feel free to add my number to your contacts." She wanted to yank the words back the minute they slipped from her lips. It was presumptuous to assume he would want to get in touch with her in the future.

"Will do."

"I suppose I should get to the reason I called so you can get back to whatever you were doing."

"You mean it wasn't just to hear my voice?" His tone was warm and friendly. "I hoped you were calling to get my day off to a smooth start."

She laughed and leaned against the porch rail. Jake was just as easy to talk to as she remembered. "That too. But the other reason was to ask if you would consider letting Molly be a mother's helper a few hours a week. The girls really had fun with her yesterday. I'll pay her, of course."

"I'll have to ask her, but I can't imagine that she'll say no. She's always telling me that she's not a kid anymore, so she'll probably be thrilled to have a job. Not to mention that she was quite enamored of your little girls. She talked about them all the way home."

"Same here. And they woke up talking about her. Apparently she's their new best friend."

"I'll talk to her and get back to you. When is the best time to call?"

Elizabeth liked that he didn't speak for his daughter, didn't accept Elizabeth's offer on Molly's behalf. That one action spoke volumes about the kind of dad that he was. "Any time. My mobile is always on."

"Good enough. We'll talk soon."

She ended the call and then turned to Gianna and Lucy, who were looking at her expectantly. "Is Molly coming over to play with us?"

"I asked her dad. He's going to talk to her and then ring me back."

The girls looked at each other and then cheered.

"We don't know that she's going to come," Elizabeth cautioned. Ten-year-olds didn't generally hang out with five-year-olds. She might not want to do that, even if she was getting paid.

"She's coming," Gianna said. "She likes us."

Elizabeth smiled. There was nothing like the confidence of a five-year-old. Even though it shouldn't have mattered one way or the other, Elizabeth hoped Jake liked her too.

Jake held his phone for a moment after they ended the call. He'd thought about Elizabeth quite a bit yesterday. She'd been the last person on his mind before he'd fallen asleep last night and the first person on his mind when he'd woken up this morning. His preoccupation with her was as troubling as it was exhilarating.

He was attracted to Elizabeth. It wasn't something that he'd expected to happen, nor was it something that he welcomed. Not that he wanted to spend the rest of his life alone. But when he decided to open his heart again, he didn't want it to be with someone who might not be in the country next month. That would be pure foolishness. The best thing to do—the *smart* thing to do—would be to keep his distance so his attraction wouldn't grow. That way he wouldn't risk being hurt when she went back to Australia.

But that was the coward's way of thinking. Did he really want to live his life avoiding all risks? Playing it safe didn't sound appealing. He could miss out on a lot of good things that way. Admittedly, he'd been devastated when Maggie had died, but even knowing how much he would suffer once he'd lost her, he wouldn't trade one moment that they'd spent together for the world.

He chuckled to himself. Talk about putting the cart before the horse. There was nothing going on between him and Elizabeth. Nor had she even hinted about wanting something to develop. All she'd done was ask if his daugh-

ter could help her with her twins. That was it. Yet his imagination had them practically walking down the aisle.

"What's so funny?" Pete asked. His son was not light
on his feet, yet Jake hadn't heard his approach. That was a
sign that he was focusing on the wrong things.

"Nothing," Jake said.

"But you were laughing. If you know a joke, you should
tell me so I can laugh too. Then I can tell my friends."

"You want to laugh, do you?" Jake grabbed his son and
then playfully tossed him onto the sofa. From the time he'd
been a toddler, Pete loved being tickled, so Jake obliged
now. Pete laughed and rolled away, then began to tickle Jake.

"I want to play," Ben said, running into the room and
jumping onto Jake's back. "Tickle me too."

"If you say so," Jake said. He flipped Ben onto the couch,
then stretched his hands in his younger son's direction,
wiggling his fingers. Ben giggled in anticipation. After
a moment, Jake tickled Ben with one hand and Pete with
the other.

Jake loved these spontaneous moments. After Maggie
had died, he had tried to schedule family fun time. It had
felt forced, and he'd thought he'd been doing something
wrong. But these unplanned times created the closeness
he'd longed for. They still had family game night and he
took the kids on scheduled excursions, but these random
moments of fun warmed his father's heart.

Maggie had been the glue that had held them all together.
More than that, she'd been the heart of the family. When
she'd died and the job had fallen to him, he'd felt incompe-
tent. Grieving, he'd fumbled around, searching for a way to
hold everyone together. Molly and Pete had been looking
to him for guidance. They'd expected him to make things
normal again. But he'd known that *normal* was a thing of

the past and wouldn't be returning. Maggie was gone, and no one could fill her shoes.

No, if he ever married again—hell, if he ever seriously got involved again—it would have to be with someone really, really special. And since in his experience women like that were one in a million, what were the chances of that happening again?

"Grab his legs, Ben!" Pete yelled as he grabbed Jake's arms.

"Okay!" Ben said. He knelt on the floor and did his best to corral Jake.

After a couple of minutes of half-hearted resistance, Jake allowed himself to be overpowered. Eventually they all ended up on the floor, laughing uproariously. Jake held up his hands in surrender. "I give—you win."

Pete and Ben cheered and then stood with their hands raised over their heads. Pete shouted, "We're the champions!"

Ben nodded. "We're the best!"

"You should never try to beat us at tickling, Dad," Pete said. "We always win."

"I know. But I won't give up. Next time I'll win."

"What are you guys doing?" Molly asked from the doorway. She was dressed in a pink T-shirt and denim shorts. She used to goof around with them, but a few months ago she'd stopped. At the same time, she'd become interested in jewelry. She'd begged him to let her get her ears pierced, but he'd said no.

According to her, all of the girls in fifth grade had pierced ears. He didn't know whether that was true or not, but he'd told her that she shouldn't follow the crowd. The glare she'd focused on him had been searing. He might not have known the right thing to say, but he'd found the wrong thing that time.

There would come a time when he'd have to say yes, but not yet. She was still too young. *WWMD* hadn't helped. He and Maggie had never discussed what age would be appropriate to let Molly get her ears pierced.

"We were tickling Dad," Pete said. "Do you want to play?"

Molly frowned and shook her head. "No. That's a boy game."

Once again Jake was assailed by guilt. Molly's interests were changing, and he had to let her know that he understood. The problem was…he didn't. Not completely. He was a guy, and no matter how hard he tried, his imagination only got him so far.

But right now there was something he could do to wipe that frown from her face. "Do you remember the twins you talked to at the Pony Club?"

She gave him a *Do you think I have memory problems?* look. "Uh, yeah. It was only yesterday."

He decided to ignore her preteen attitude. "I talked to their mother. She said they really liked you. So she wants to know if you'll be interested in helping her with the girls a few hours a week. She said she'll pay you."

Molly grinned. "You mean like a real job?"

"Yes. I told her that I'd ask you."

"Yes. I want to. Of course I want to. I liked Lucy and Gianna a lot. They're only five, but they're fun to be around."

"I'll call her and let her know."

"Tell her that I can come every day."

"I don't think she'll need your help that often."

Molly was hugging herself and turning in circles, so Jake was certain that she hadn't heard his last comment. He and Elizabeth could work out the details later. The idea of talking to her again made Jake want to hug himself and turn in circles too. He made do with a smile.

"Can you call her now?" Molly asked once she stopped celebrating.

"Absolutely." Jake pulled up the most recent number on his call list and dialed it.

Molly held out her hand for the phone. "I should probably be the one to talk to her, since it's my job."

Jake nodded, tamping down his disappointment at being robbed of the opportunity to hear Elizabeth's voice again.

Molly held the phone to her ear. "Hi. This is Molly Mc-Creery. My dad told me that you want me to help with Lucy and Gianna." She stared at Jake and her brothers, her message clear: *Go away.* When they didn't move fast enough to suit her, she turned her back on them and walked over to the windows.

"Come on, guys," Jake said, dropping an arm over his sons' shoulders and steering them from the room. "Let's give your sister some privacy."

"We don't want to listen to her conversation anyway," Pete said, clearly offended.

"Yeah," Ben echoed. "We don't want to listen to her conversation."

Despite their protests, they were walking so slowly a snail could beat them in a foot race.

"Would you please hold on?" Molly said, giving them a meaningful look. Despite feeling put out, Jake was impressed by the way she was conducting business. He'd worn that expression and said those words countless times himself. This was the second time in as many days that he'd heard his words coming from the mouths of his children.

"You can walk faster than that," Jake said, nudging his sons.

Pete and Ben picked up the pace. By the time they reached the kitchen, they'd lost interest in trying to overhear the phone call. Pete opened the refrigerator and stared into it as if he hadn't finished eating breakfast less than thirty minutes ago. When nothing appealed to him, he closed the door.

After a moment, Pete and Ben headed for their room to play.

Jake was wiping off the counter when Molly ran into the room. She held out the phone to him. "Elizabeth wants to talk to you."

"Okay." His palms suddenly felt damp, and he rubbed them over his jeans. This was ridiculous. He wasn't some teenager about to talk to his crush. He was thirty-eight years old and a father. Nevertheless, he took extra pains to control his voice. "This is Jake."

"Hi. Thanks for allowing me to talk to Molly. She is such a sweet girl and very professional."

"That she is," Jake said proudly.

"Molly accepted my offer to be my mother's helper. My girls think they'll be having a playdate. And in a way they will, although I was careful not to refer to it that way to Molly. I'll be here the entire time, so you don't need to worry about supervision."

"When would you like for her to start?"

"How about tomorrow? I think I can hold the girls off until then." She laughed softly, and the sound illuminated a dark place inside him.

"That sounds like a plan."

She gave him directions to the cabin. He was familiar with the area.

Elizabeth insisted on paying Molly minimum wage. "After all, we want to teach her not to undervalue herself."

He liked the way Elizabeth said *we*. As if they were a team. He'd been alone on this parenting journey for six years, so even the illusion of having a partner was comforting.

"What time are we going tomorrow?" Molly asked the second he'd ended the call.

"Tomorrow around eleven. We'll drop the boys off at karate first and then go over to Elizabeth's cabin. Does that work for you?"

She grinned. "This is going to be so good. Now I need to go pick out my clothes."

"What for? You're going to be playing with Lucy and Gianna. I'm sure whatever you wear will be fine."

Molly gave him a look that he was seeing much too often—the one that made it clear he didn't understand her at all. He hated that feeling, but he was coming to believe that it was true. The older his daughter became, the less he was able to relate to her. He wasn't going to turn into the stereotypical single dad who couldn't find common ground with his daughter. Underneath the attitude she was still his little Molly. He just needed to try harder.

"Do you want help?"

"Dad," she said, "I know how to pick out my own clothes."

"Right."

He was a bit disappointed at being brushed aside, but even that couldn't stop him from being excited.

He was going to see Elizabeth again tomorrow.

Chapter Three

Elizabeth checked her appearance in the full-size mirror, turning from side to side to make sure she looked her best from every angle. When she realized what she was doing, she laughed at herself and went into the main room where the girls were playing. This wasn't a date. She wasn't even leaving the house. She was simply entertaining a ten-year-old girl. The fact that said child was being dropped off by her handsome father was immaterial. Besides, she doubted Jake would give her more than a passing glance. She didn't get the impression that he was interested in romance. Given her situation, neither was she.

When Jake had told her that Molly was the only girl in the household, her heart had gone out to the child. With four sisters, Elizabeth couldn't picture being the only girl in the family. She supposed it would be lonely at times. She couldn't fathom not having a sister to share secrets with or talk to about fashion and boys. Elizabeth couldn't provide Molly with a female sibling, but she could give her two little girls to play with. Although Gianna and Lucy were friendly, they hadn't made a friend in Bronco yet. Until Molly. So this was Elizabeth's opportunity to help Molly and the twins at the same time.

There was a knock on the door, and Gianna and Lucy

hopped up and raced through the room ahead of Elizabeth. When they reached the door, they stopped short of opening it. They knew the rule: they could peep out the side window, but only Elizabeth could open the door.

"It's Molly," Gianna said, tugging on the bottom of Elizabeth's shorts, urging her to move quickly.

Lucy applauded and jumped up and down.

"I know," Elizabeth said. She opened the door and stepped aside. The three girls squealed with glee as if they were long lost friends who'd been parted for years.

Gianna and Lucy grabbed Molly by the hand and tugged her into the cabin. Not that they had to exert much pressure. Molly seemed just as eager to come inside as they were to have her.

Elizabeth and Jake glanced at each other, sharing amused smiles. When their eyes met, Elizabeth's stomach went all topsy-turvy. What in the world was that? This was the second time her body had acted like a teenager around Jake. Arlo had been her one and only, so this reaction shocked her into stillness. The girls' excited chatter shook her out of her stupor, and she remembered her manners.

"Won't you come in and have a cuppa?" Elizabeth asked Jake, who hadn't crossed the threshold. "I mean coffee. I grew up in America, but I've lived in Australia for ten years. At times I have to remind myself to use American English."

"I understand," Jake said. "I wish I could stay, but I can't. I dropped the boys at karate before I came here. I need to get back before class ends."

Elizabeth held her smile in place to cover her disappointment. She'd hoped to have a bit of adult time. No, that wasn't entirely honest. She'd hoped to have a bit of *Jake* time. She'd been looking forward to getting to know him better. This playdate had seemed like the perfect no-pressure opportunity. "Okay. Maybe another time."

Jake checked his watch and then looked at her. "I suppose I have a few minutes. And a cup of coffee sounds good."

"Come on in. I'll brew some."

They stepped into the main room. Molly had made herself right at home and was brushing a doll's hair. Gianna and Lucy had brought several of their favorite dolls from home. Elizabeth's sisters and cousins had gifted them with more, so there was no shortage of dolls. At least fifteen were lined up on the sofa.

"We're going into the kitchen," Elizabeth said.

"We'll be fine," Molly said.

"I'm sure you will."

The girls didn't give her another look before returning their attention to their dolls. Apparently her presence was no longer necessary.

"Have a seat," Elizabeth said, gesturing to the kitchen table. She grabbed the coffee beans and began to grind them.

"Thanks. I appreciate you allowing Molly to come over today. When she was younger, she used to want to hang out with me and her brothers. Seemingly overnight she went from being one of the guys to moving to her own little island where we aren't welcome."

"Don't take it personally. She's a tween girl. It's only natural for her to develop other interests."

"I asked her if she wanted to bring a doll with her, and let me tell you…" Jake grimaced and shook his head ruefully. "The glare she sent me could have burned a hole in my chest. But now she's in there playing with dolls. I just don't get it."

"Tween, remember? She's in between being a little girl and a teenager. Besides, she's being a mother's helper. She's keeping my girls entertained by playing dolls with them. It's a subtle distinction, but it's there."

"If you say so."

"Believe me, she doesn't need to bring toys with her. My girls have plenty. My entire family is doing everything in their power to convince me to stay in Bronco. To their way of thinking, everything is fair game. Including bribes. They believe if they win over the girls, I'll fall in line."

"I thought you were on vacation. Are you thinking about moving to Bronco?"

Elizabeth shrugged. She set the beans in the coffeemaker and let them brew. Although she preferred the sweeter, fancier Australian drink, she figured Jake would prefer the familiar American coffee. "I don't know. I'm at a crossroads in my life, so nothing is out of the realm of possibility. I want to do what's best for my girls. I'm just not sure whether that is moving to Bronco or going back home to Australia."

She glanced at Jake, and he nodded.

"Yesterday was the first day the girls didn't ask when we were going back home. Before we came here, I told them that we were going on a vacation. This isn't what they expected. They're used to ocean vacations where they can play on the beach and swim."

"There aren't many beaches in Montana."

"I know." She grabbed two mugs, filled them with coffee, and handed one to Jake. "Cream and sugar?"

He shook his head. "I take mine black."

Suppressing a shudder, Elizabeth added milk and sugar to hers. Not exactly a flat white, but this would do for now.

She sat across from Jake and glanced at him over her cup. Dressed casually in jeans and a blue shirt, he appeared totally at ease.

"Yesterday, I heard your son mention that you were a widower."

Jake nodded slowly. "Yes."

"I'm sorry for your loss."

"Thank you."

Elizabeth glanced at her hands. She inhaled deeply and slowly exhaled. "My husband, Arlo, died suddenly two years ago."

"I'm sorry."

"Does it ever let up?"

"The pain?"

She nodded, unable to speak.

He sipped his coffee, clearly thinking about how to answer her. "That's a good question. I don't know if the pain eases or if you eventually learn how to live with it. I have three kids, so I can't just wallow in misery. After Maggie died, I had no choice but to get on with my life the best way I knew how." He took another swallow of his coffee and frowned. "Sorry. I know that isn't much help. And probably not what you wanted to hear. I guess all I can say is that you have to keep going. Just put one foot in front of the other."

"Actually, that sums up how I feel. Making it from morning to night is a win for me. People seem anxious for me to remarry for my girls' sakes. And maybe for theirs too. Remarrying will be a sign that I'm no longer in pain, so they don't have to worry about me. They don't seem to believe that my girls and I are a complete family. A different family than we were when my husband was alive, and not the kind of family I'd dreamed of being, but a family nonetheless. And we are fine."

Jake nodded, then grinned wryly. "I won't bore you with the horror stories of the women who started coming around a couple of months after my wife's death."

"Yikes. Thankfully I didn't have that experience. Men were inclined to keep their distance and let me mourn the loss of my husband." They didn't speak for a minute, but the silence wasn't uneasy. And it gave them each a chance to deal with the sad emotions they'd dredged up. Any other time Elizabeth would have sat quietly, but she wouldn't get to know him better that way. And for a reason she wasn't quite ready to face, she wanted to get to know him better.

"Now that we've established there's not an ocean in the vicinity, what do you do for fun?" she asked, returning to the earlier, happier topic.

Jake smiled, apparently sharing her desire to change the subject. "Are you asking Jake the man or Jake the single father? Because my answers would be vastly different."

"Either. Both."

"Well, I'm a rancher, so I'm always busy, but when it's me and the kids we like to spend time outside. We love packing up sleeping bags and spending the night on the range under the stars. They still get a kick out of cooking hot dogs over a campfire. Especially Ben, who's only six and finally gets to hold his own fork."

"I can imagine how thrilling that is for him."

"He tries to keep up with Pete. He wants to be a big boy."

Elizabeth nodded. "I know how that feels."

He inhaled, and Elizabeth's gaze was drawn to his massive chest. She longed to run her fingers over it just to see if it was as hard as it looked. "I'm proud of him for wanting to do things for himself, but I'm sorry to see him grow up so fast. I miss the baby years. Given how hard it was to take care of him without Maggie—those early days and nights were rough—I should want to see him growing up." He shook his head. "This feeling is ridiculous."

"But completely understandable," she said. "My girls

were only three when we lost their dad. I don't have to tell you how hard those days were—even with lots of help from my in-laws and friends. Lucy and Gianna are becoming more independent, which is good. Even so, a part of me misses the days when I could hold both my little girls on my lap and just cuddle them. Don't get me wrong, we still do some of that. And every once in a while, they revert to some of their baby ways. But they're growing up so fast. I'm conflicted." She sighed and put her feelings aside. "So what does Jake the man do for fun?"

"Provided I have a babysitter?"

"Yes," she said. "In a perfect world, what does a night of fun look like?"

"I'm a bit of a foodie."

"Do you mean more than steak and potatoes?"

"At the risk of being forced to turn in my rancher card, yes. I love all kinds of foods. Whenever I can, I try out a different restaurant that serves authentic cuisine from different cultures."

"Do you prefer any particular kinds? Or are there foods that you avoid?"

"Nah, I'll try anything," he said. "Why veto something without giving it a try first? I don't want to miss a delicacy simply because it doesn't look like what I'm used to."

Elizabeth smiled. "I like your style."

Jake's watch beeped. He sighed, then lifted his cup and finished the rest of his drink. Standing, he pushed the chair under the table and put his mug in the sink. "I need to get going—I don't want to be late picking up the boys. Thanks for the coffee."

Time certainly had flown. She stood too. "I enjoyed the company."

When they entered the main room, Molly was sitting between the girls on a comfy chair. She was spinning a tale about a princess and her favorite pony. Gianna and Lucy were totally entranced and didn't look up when the adults entered. If today was anything to go by, this was going to work out wonderfully.

"Are you going to pick up Ben and Pete now?" Molly asked.

"Yes," Jake said.

"Okay. Bye." She smiled and then went back to her story. Jake blinked.

Elizabeth sympathized with him. He'd just shared his mixed feelings about watching his younger son grow up. It was probably even more difficult with his one and only daughter. "She'll be fine."

"I know. She's had playdates before. I don't know why this feels different."

"Because it is different. She's at work." Elizabeth flashed him a grin. "Your daughter has a job. She's growing up."

He laughed. "And I'm being silly. What time do you want me to pick her up?"

"Whenever you want. I don't have any plans."

She opened the front door, and he hesitated as if unsure what to do. She suffered from the same confusion—which was ridiculous. This hadn't been a date, so there was no need to decide whether they should kiss. So why did she feel disappointed when he jogged down the stairs, hopped into his SUV, and drove away?

Jake tried to keep his mind on the road as he drove to the dojo in town. Yet no matter how hard he tried to concentrate, his mind kept straying to Elizabeth. Dressed in denim cutoffs and a blouse that she'd tied around her waist, she'd looked casual and glamorous all at once. She was too appealing for his own good, which was why he'd made up his mind to keep her at a distance. He'd intended to drop off Molly and leave, but when he'd seen the disappointed look on Elizabeth's face as he'd turned down her invitation for coffee, he'd known he couldn't stick with his plan.

He didn't regret the time he'd spent with her. It had been pure pleasure. She was even more delightful than he'd remembered. He was glad to learn that her time in Bronco might become permanent. But, he reminded himself, she could just as easily return to Australia.

Traffic was light, and he arrived at the dojo with three minutes to spare. He jumped from the SUV and made it inside in time to see his sons bow to the sensei. Once class was dismissed, the assembled kids raced over to their parents.

"Hey, Dad. Did you see us?" Ben asked.

"Sorry, bud. I missed the class. But I'll see you next time."

"It's okay," he said easily. "We just did the same things we always do."

"Just better?" Jake asked.

The boy shrugged and rubbed his nose. "You need to ask sensei about that."

Jake laughed. Ben was nothing if not honest.

"So is Molly still at her job?" Pete asked.

"Yes."

"What is she doing?"

"When I left she was telling Lucy and Gianna a story and playing with dolls."

"And she's getting paid for that?" he asked, his voice a cross between outrage and disbelief. "I can get a job doing that. Maybe their mom will let me help her too."

"You want to play with dolls?" Ben asked.

"No."

"Well, that's part of the job," Jake said.

"Never mind," Pete said, heaving a heavy sigh.

Jake nodded, hoping this was the end of it. Pete had never had a problem with Molly being able to do things that he couldn't before, so his attitude was perplexing. Hopefully this wasn't the beginning of the dreaded sibling rivalry. It was difficult enough dealing with Molly's changing interests and preteen snark.

The boys raced to the locker room to change into their street clothes. They returned a couple of minutes later, their gi tucked beneath their arms, folded as neatly as eight- and six-year-olds could manage. One of the first things their sensei had stressed was the importance of respect. That respect extended to their clothes. Each of the boys had taken his words seriously and never wore their gi outside of class.

Once they were buckled in the SUV, Pete asked, "What time are we picking up Molly?"

"Good question. How about we get her now?" Elizabeth wanted help for a few hours a week. Jake didn't think she meant all at once. Besides, this was Molly's first day at work, and he didn't want her to get tired. That last thought was a stretch. Molly thrived on having younger kids around to care for, so no doubt she was in seventh heaven.

He'd told Molly more than once that it wasn't her job to look after her brothers—it was his. She'd said that she understood, yet that hadn't stopped her from hovering.

As Jake drove, he listened with one ear to the conversation Pete and Ben were having about one of their favorite cartoons while taking in the surroundings. Though he lived in the area all of his life, he was still struck by the sheer beauty of nature in and around Bronco. The green grass, blue sky, and mountains in the distance were as soothing as they were picturesque. Just looking at them diminished his worries and filled him with a sense of calm.

Elizabeth's cabin was located on a beautiful plot of land. Or rather, her *sister's* cabin. The fact that she was staying in a borrowed home amplified the temporary nature of her visit. She was in town for vacation. When it ended as all vacations did, she would probably return to her home on the other side of the world. He reminded himself of his decision to keep his emotional distance from her—if not his physical distance—but somehow he didn't hear the warning. Despite everything, he didn't want to keep her at arm's length. He'd believed he'd buried his interest in women and his heart with Maggie. Now he was discovering that wasn't the case.

Too bad the first woman he was interested in lived in Australia.

He pulled in front of the cabin. Before he could turn off the engine, the boys had jumped from the SUV and were wandering around.

"This place is cool," Pete said. He bent down and then stood, a toad in his hand. Toads were rare in Montana, so Jake was surprised to see one. "They have lots of cool animals."

"Can we take it home?" Ben asked.

"No," Jake said instantly. If it was up to the boys, the house would be a menagerie. They wanted to keep every animal or bug they saw.

"Why not?"

"His friends and family live here," Jake said. "He'll be lonely if we take him away from them."

"We can find them and bring them too," Ben said.

"This is his home. He wouldn't feel comfortable in a strange place." Those words instantly made him think of Elizabeth. Even though she'd been born and raised in America, she lived in Australia now. She'd given birth to her children there. How strange Montana must seem after all that time away. Perhaps she needed a friend to help her get acclimated. He shoved the idea aside. His life was busy enough. He didn't need to seek out more tasks to fill what little time he had.

"Okay." Pete set the toad back on the ground, and they watched as it hopped away, vanishing into the tall grass. The kids raced to the door and knocked on it loudly.

"I think they heard you," Jake said dryly.

The door swung open. He glanced up and straight into Elizabeth's large brown eyes. They twinkled with amusement. "Hello, boys. Come on in."

"Thank you," Pete said politely. Apparently Jake's lessons on manners were getting through.

"Thank you," Ben echoed. He looked into Elizabeth's face and smiled. "You're really pretty. Isn't she pretty, Daddy?"

Jake stuttered, temporarily unsure how to answer that question. The easy answer was *yes*. Because Elizabeth was gorgeous. "Remember what I said about commenting on people's appearance, Ben. It's rude."

"But I thought you meant we couldn't say bad things. We can't say good things either?" The boy sounded so perplexed that Jake struggled not to laugh.

"Thank you for the compliment, Ben," Elizabeth said.

"You're welcome," he said and then turned to look at Jake. "See, Daddy? She didn't mind me calling her pretty."

He could only sigh as Ben joined the other kids in the cabin's main room.

"You're going to have your hands full with that one," Elizabeth said, grinning.

"Don't I know it," Jake replied. The noise level coming

from the front room rose several decibels with the addition of the two boys. Pete and Ben simultaneously questioned the girls about their day and showed off what they'd learned in karate.

"How about a snack?" Elizabeth asked.

That quieted the room.

"Can we have biscuits?" Gianna asked.

"What kind of snack is a biscuit?" Ben asked.

"The best kind," she said. "Don't you like biscuits?"

"For breakfast," Pete said.

"You get to eat biscuits for breakfast?" Lucy asked, amazed.

Elizabeth laughed and tugged on one of her daughter's long braids. "Biscuits are something different here than at home."

"Oh."

Elizabeth then looked at Jake's three kids. "What we call biscuits in Australia, you call cookies. So, would you like some cookies?"

"Yes!" Pete exclaimed, jumping to his feet.

"We love cookies," Ben said, coming to stand beside Elizabeth. He took her hand and swung it back and forth. There was a look of pure adoration on his face. Jake had never seen his son look like that at anyone, and his heart ached. Without a doubt, Ben would have adored Maggie. And she would have adored him right back.

"Then everyone go wash your hands," Elizabeth said, "and meet me in the kitchen."

If possible, the racket the kids made was even louder. Only Lucy seemed to lag behind.

"What's wrong, sweetie?" Elizabeth asked, stooping down so she could look into her daughter's eyes.

Lucy shrugged.

"Too much noise?" Jake asked. He squatted down beside Elizabeth so he too was at eye level with Lucy.

"Maybe," she said slowly.

"Perhaps I should get my kids and leave," Jake suggested to Elizabeth. He didn't want Lucy to feel uncomfortable in her own home. Clearly she wasn't used to such rambunctious kids as his boys.

"Molly too?" Lucy asked.

"Yes, she's one of my kids."

"I like Molly. I don't want her to go home." Lucy frowned as if in thought. "I suppose the boys can stay too."

"Are you sure?" Jake asked. "Molly will still be your friend even if we don't stay. You can play with her another day."

"I'm sure. The boys are okay. I guess I like them too."

With that proclamation, Lucy ran off to wash her hands.

"We can still leave," Jake offered.

Elizabeth shook her head. "There's no need to do that. Lucy might take a bit more time to make up her mind, but once she's reached a decision, she's comfortable with it. I want her to know that I respect her choice. I don't want to overrule her unless it's a matter of safety."

"In that case, I'm looking forward to having a biscuit."

Elizabeth laughed and punched his shoulder. They were still squatting, and their eyes met. And held. The amusement in hers gradually faded, morphing into something that resembled desire. She blinked, and the look was gone. That was probably for the best.

One side of her lip lifted in a sexy curve as she rose to her full height. She was about five feet eight, a few inches shorter than his six feet.

He stood as well and followed her into the kitchen. It was small, but with seven people inside it was positively claustrophobic. The kids didn't seem to mind. They were sitting around the table—Lucy and Gianna were sharing a chair, and Ben and Molly were sharing another. Pete had his own. He looked up and smiled. "We left a chair for you guys."

"Thanks," Jake said. The idea of sharing a chair with Elizabeth held more than a little appeal, but he wasn't sure she would feel the same. "I don't mind standing."

Pete shrugged as if it didn't matter one way or the other to him.

Elizabeth doled out the cookies to the kids and then looked at Jake. "What kind would you like?"

"I think I'll try a mint."

To be honest, any kind would do. He was happy just to be spending time with Elizabeth. He couldn't exactly call this a quiet moment, although there was a lot less noise now that the kids were filling their mouths with cookies and drinking the milk that Elizabeth had poured to wash them down, but it was still peaceful and fulfilling. He was learning to appreciate the small moments that he and the kids spent together. Life wasn't filled with the big, exciting moments that often formed memories. It was made up of the regular day-to-day interactions. These were the moments that set the tone for their childhoods and would give them the confidence they needed to navigate the future. These times determined whether his kids would look back and say they'd had a happy childhood.

"I think you're going to like it," Elizabeth said with a bright smile. He noticed that she smiled easily. He liked that about her. Although life had dealt her a raw hand, she hadn't let it make her bitter. But then, with two small children, she didn't have a choice other than to roll with the punches. Even so, he wondered what she felt in the still of the night. When she was alone in her bed, did she reach out for her husband's side of the bed, hoping to encounter his sleeping form, as Jake occasionally did, hoping to touch Maggie? Did she have conversations with him in her mind? Did she ask herself what he would think of her choices?

When he realized he was standing there with his cookie in his hand, he took a bite. "Wow. That's good."

"I knew you would like it," Elizabeth said as she sat down.

"You should sit down with Mummy," Gianna said. "The chair is big enough for two people."

"And you always tell us not to eat standing up," Molly added. "You don't want to drop crumbs on the floor for somebody else to have to clean up."

What was it with his kids throwing his words back in his face?

He glanced at Elizabeth. Their eyes met and sexual tension singed the air. Without breaking their gazes, she slid to one side of the chair. Heart pounding, Jake crossed the room and eased into the chair beside her. Despite what Gianna claimed, the chair was definitely not made for two people.

Even though Elizabeth had moved over, their thighs still touched. The heat from her bare thigh worked its way through the denim covering his. Her sweet scent wafted around him, and the temptation to kiss her spouted out of nowhere. Knowing that would be totally improper, he took a second bite of his cookie. It was good, but not as good as kissing Elizabeth would be. But since that was out of the question, he needed to think about something else. "What kind of cookies are these?"

"They're biscuits," Lucy corrected.

"Right. I forgot. What kind of biscuits are these?" he asked.

"Tim Tams. They're Australia's most popular brand,"

Elizabeth said. She gave him a wicked grin as if she knew about his struggle. Perhaps she shared it.

Feeling a bit mischievous, he leaned a bit closer and was pleased when she inhaled and her eyes widened. Not wanting to attract the kids' attention, he replied, "I can see why. We might need to visit there so we can have more of these."

"You'll like it there," Gianna told him before turning to look at Molly. "If you come home with us, you'll be able to see our room."

"And play on our swings," Lucy added.

"Are we really going?" Molly asked, and Jake realized belatedly that none of the children had picked up on his joking tone. More than that, Lucy's and Gianna's words reminded him that Elizabeth and her little family were only going to be in the United States for a short while.

"I never like to say never," he said. "But we don't have any plans to visit Australia right now."

"It would be cool if we went," Pete said. "Then we could get a pet kangaroo. Or a koala bear. They have those in Australia. We read a book about them in school."

"I'll keep that in mind," Jake said.

"If you like Tim Tams, you don't have to go that far to get them," Elizabeth said. "They're sold in some stores here in the States. I'm not promising they have them here in Montana, though."

As the kids then began to talk about other things, Jake whispered to Elizabeth, "Thanks for the save."

"No worries. I sometimes forget how easily a joke can be misinterpreted. Before I know it, the girls are off and running with it."

"I'm usually more careful," he said.

"I understand," she said. "The first time I tasted a Tim Tam I nearly screamed. It was just that good."

Maybe. But it wasn't the delicious flavor of the treat that had distracted him. It was her. It felt so natural to be in her company. Hanging out with the kids. Like one big happy family.

What was he thinking? They'd hardly spent any time together. Their friendship—if they actually were friends—was too new. The last thing he needed was a thought like that.

He threw his napkin into the trash can. "C'mon, kids. It's time to go home." He had to get out of there before he said or did something stupid.

"Aww, but we just got here," Ben whined. The other kids chorused in with similar complaints.

"We can't monopolize Elizabeth and the twins' day," Jake said.

"I don't even know what that means, so how can I be doing it?" Ben asked.

Elizabeth laughed. It was a sweet sound that made Jake's pulse race. He could get used to that sound. Of course, he wouldn't let himself.

"It means that we need to leave so they can do what they planned to do for the rest of the day."

"Oh."

"Me too?" Molly asked. "Because I'm at work."

"You too." When she frowned, he hastened to add, "But if Elizabeth and the girls are free this weekend, they can come over for a cookout."

All eyes swung from him to Elizabeth. The kids seemed to be holding their collective breaths as they waited for her response. When Jake realized that he was holding his breath too, he forced himself to exhale. He was putting way too much importance on this spur-of-the-moment invitation.

"I would love to come," she said. "What do you think, Lucy and Gianna? Would you like to visit Molly's house?"

"Yes," they exclaimed without hesitation.

Elizabeth shifted her gaze back to Jake. Her radiant smile widened, and his heart thumped in response. "We would love to visit you this weekend. Do you need us to bring anything?"

"You can bring more of these cookies," Pete said. "They're really good."

Jake shook his head at his son. "Pete."

"What? She asked."

"I did ask," Elizabeth pointed out.

"That won't be necessary. Your company will be all that we need. How does Saturday work for you? I'll throw something on the grill for dinner."

"That sounds wonderful. We'll be there."

"Good." He smiled, for the moment quieting the voice inside him that warned he was getting too close to Elizabeth. "Then it's a date."

Chapter Four

It's a date.

The words echoed in Elizabeth's mind as she helped Jake hustle his kids out the door and into his SUV. There was a lot of commotion as the kids stopped walking to say *one last thing*. What should have been a two-minute goodbye took nearly five times that long as the children kept finding unique ways to stall. The noise and laughter weren't distracting enough to stop Elizabeth from replaying Jake's words in her mind.

It's a date.

She knew he hadn't meant the word in the traditional sense. Nobody took five kids on a date. Even so, she couldn't stop the tingling sensation that shot through her body each time she thought of his words. And she couldn't stop thinking of them.

It was strange. On the outside, everything seemed normal. She was sure nobody could tell how affected she was simply by looking at her. She smiled and laughed with the kids, making appropriate responses to their questions and comments. But on the inside? Butterflies were flitting around her stomach, crashing into the walls before turning and flying in the other direction.

Not that she should've been worried about Jake sensing her turmoil. He would have to know her better and longer to do that. Since they were still getting to know each other, she didn't have to worry that he could know that his simple statement had turned her into a ball of nerves.

Finally Jake corralled his three and got them into his SUV. Elizabeth stood between Lucy and Gianna beside the stairs. They waved as Jake drove off.

"See you on Saturday!" Molly yelled from the front passenger window.

"Bye!" Lucy and Gianna called. The girls waved until Jake's vehicle had driven out of sight.

"How many days until Saturday?" Lucy asked.

"You remember the days-of-the-week song?" Elizabeth asked. Even though the girls were too young for school, Elizabeth taught them at home. They could count to one hundred, print their first and last names, recognize their colors, and read basic sight words. They would be ready for school whether that was here in Montana or back home in Australia.

Lucy and Gianna nodded and then began to sing. As they recited the days of the week, they raised a finger with each day. By the time they reached Saturday, they each had seven fingers raised. Elizabeth laughed. That wasn't right. Of course, since they had started with Sunday, there was nothing they could do but have seven.

"Today is Monday. So let's try that again."

When they reached Saturday, they were each holding five fingers in the air.

"Five?" Gianna asked tentatively.

"That's right."

"That's a long time," Lucy whined.

"I know. But we'll have lots of fun between now and then."

"Doing what?"

"Playing. Going around town. And we'll visit my sisters and cousins. Doesn't that sound like fun?"

The girls exchanged glances. To them, Elizabeth's family were a bunch of strangers. They'd spent time with them on several occasions during this visit, but her daughters weren't of an age where they had much fun with adults. Even those bearing piles of gifts. Though Tori had come to Australia last year, the girls had been even younger then. Much too young to form a close relationship. In fact, they barely remembered her or her visit. Knowing her girls didn't feel close to her family hurt Elizabeth's heart. Before she'd moved halfway across the world, she'd spent a lot of time with her immediate and extended family. They'd been as close as a family could be.

Their bonds had been tested when Elizabeth moved to Australia ten years ago, but they'd held despite her absence. She and her family had picked up where they'd left off. But Lucy and Gianna didn't have a lifetime of shared memories to draw on. Their memories were of Australia and the friends and family, including Elizabeth's sister Carly, they had there. It would take time spent together for them to grow close to their American family.

But did Elizabeth intend to stay here, or was she going to take her children and go back home? Would growing close to her American family come at the cost of their relationships to their Australian family, who were their last links to Arlo? Those questions kept her awake some nights.

They weren't the only cause of her restlessness. Thoughts of Jake had also disturbed her sleep last night.

She would be lying if she denied being attracted to Jake. There was something about him that appealed to her on a basic level. Truth be told, a simple sexual attraction would be preferable. Those feelings were shallow and generally didn't survive long. But her attraction was also emotional. She didn't like it and fought her hardest to resist it. But there was something about his kindness and patience that reached inside her heart. She felt comfortable with him and looked forward to spending more time with him.

The very notion was a betrayal of Arlo's memory and all they'd shared. How could she possibly feel something—anything—for another man? Arlo Freeman had been her one true love. The first time she'd laid eyes on him she'd known that he would own her heart for all time. Even two years since his death, her heart still called out for him. The idea that she could suddenly care for Jake was unimaginable.

Though she knew that was illogical, she couldn't stop believing it was wrong to like Jake and want to spend time with him. It wasn't as if they would be alone. Despite what he'd said, they weren't going on a date. She and the girls were visiting him and his kids on his ranch. The twins hadn't met many kids in Montana yet, so Elizabeth was happy they liked Jake's kids so much. Her girls weren't used to isolation. They needed other playmates.

"I like Molly," Lucy said, confirming Elizabeth's thought.

"I know," she said.

"Did you know her mum died?" Gianna asked.

"Yes."

"That's sad," Gianna added. "She died a long time ago. She's in Heaven now."

"I know."

"Just like Daddy," Lucy said.

"I miss Daddy," Gianna said. "I wish he could come back from Heaven."

"Me too," Lucy said.

And just like that, Elizabeth knew it would be unthinkable to even consider starting a relationship with Jake. It would further complicate their already complicated lives. They each had young children who had lost a parent. They might not still be mourning, but that didn't mean they were ready and able to welcome another person into their lives.

Adding new Hawkins relatives was enough of a change for Lucy and Gianna.

Elizabeth gathered her daughters into her arms and held them close, trying her best to let her love surround them and soothe their hurt. It could not replace Arlo's love or presence, but nothing could. Just as the Hawkins relatives would not replace their Australian family. The girls loved their grandparents and their uncle Nick, Arlo's older brother. And the Freemans adored them. Although they'd FaceTimed over the past weeks, Elizabeth knew it wasn't the same as spending time together. The distance between them made the impromptu visits they'd all been accustomed to impossible. At some point, the relationships would suffer and a link to Arlo would be broken.

Even so, none of them had protested when Elizabeth had informed them of her open-ended visit to America.

You need to do what you believe is best for you and your daughters, Arlo's mother, Grace, had told her. *Of course, we hope that means coming back to Australia to live. But you won't know for sure what you want unless you go back to America for a while.*

Elizabeth didn't know what she expected to happen by being back in America, but she certainly hadn't expected to become attracted to a man. A small part of her had hoped that being back home would be magical. That the answers to her future would come to her. She didn't need to know the whole plan. One or two steps would suffice for now. So far no part of the plan had been revealed.

One thing was certain—she didn't want to do anything to harm her children. She'd heard a million times that kids were resilient, but she didn't believe that was true. Lucy and Gianna had been devastated when Arlo died. But they'd been young and hadn't possessed the vocabulary to express the depth of their pain. They hadn't known the words to ask their questions or tell anyone how sad they'd been. What others had interpreted as resilience Elizabeth had recognized as confusion, hurt.

They had never known anyone who'd died, so they hadn't understood that Arlo would not be coming back from Heaven. Their paternal grandparents weren't rodeo performers, so when Elizabeth and Arlo hadn't been competing, they'd all spent time together. The girls had gotten used to not seeing their grandparents for extended periods of time while they'd traveled with their parents. But they'd known they would be together again. Long absences followed by happy reunions had been accepted as a natural part of life.

Although the twins now understood that Arlo was not coming back, they had no idea of the magnitude of their loss. Arlo had been a great father. Perhaps the best ever. He would have been an even greater one in the future if he hadn't been robbed of that chance.

"I miss Daddy too," Elizabeth said. "Do you want to look through the Daddy book?"

Arlo had always been big on taking pictures. The first time he and Elizabeth had gone out, he'd taken their picture. He'd said he'd wanted to document the first date with the woman he was going to spend the rest of his life with. He hadn't waited until they'd been doing something noteworthy to pull out his phone and snap a few shots. There were as many photos of them walking along the beach or cooking breakfast as there were of rodeo competitions and fancy events. Unlike most people, Arlo had actually printed his photos. As a result, they had numerous albums filled with memories. When the girls had been born, he'd doubled his efforts. There were many pictures of the four of them together doing everything from swimming or riding horses to sitting around watching kids' movies.

After Arlo's death, Elizabeth had taken over as family documentarian, trying to capture as many moments as Arlo had. She'd taken enough pictures to fill countless albums. She'd also devoted one album exclusively to photos of Arlo. Initially the girls had wanted to look through that album all of the time, touching Arlo's face in every picture. Over time, the request to look at the book had diminished until the album went months without being opened. Elizabeth couldn't decide if that was a good thing or not.

"No," Lucy said. "I just want to play. Can we stay out here for a while?"

Elizabeth nodded as she tried to ignore the crack that had suddenly opened up in her heart. She didn't want her daughters to mourn forever, but she didn't want them to forget Arlo either. They'd been so young when he'd died, and she knew that they had very few memories of him. She'd tried to keep him alive for them, but she knew eventually they would forget the feel of his strong arms holding them and the sound of his laughter. He would simply become a name and a face in the photographs.

Would Jake's presence—no matter how innocuous—hasten that process? Not that she needed to think too much about that. Because despite her many questions, she was certain about one thing. She wasn't ready to move on.

"Do you have enough hamburgers and buns?" Molly asked Jake. He looked up from his place at the kitchen table and met her eyes. Every once in a while, she seemed to forget that he was the father and she was the child. This was one of those times.

"Yes. You were with me when I went shopping, remember?"

She grinned sheepishly. "Oh, yeah. I forgot."

"Relax," Jake said. "Everything is going to be fine. We have plenty of food and drinks. Enough snacks for ten kids. We have whatever they might want."

"Not everything," Molly pointed out. "I wish we could have found some of those cookies they had. They were really good."

"I do too. But we have cookies of our own. Maybe Lucy and Gianna have never eaten those. Today could be their chance to try them, along with an old-fashioned American barbecue."

Her eyes lit up and she smiled. "I hadn't thought of that. We'll let them try some of my favorites."

As she raced over to the pantry and pulled out several closed packages of cookies. "I should have made some of my specialty cookies like I did for the Valentine's Day bake-off."

"Your double fudge peanut butter cookies are terrific. Maybe you can make them another time," Jake suggested.

"Okay." She was wearing her favorite shorts outfit and new sandals. She'd brushed her hair until it shone. She blew out a breath. "I'll go check and see what the boys are doing."

"Why?"

"Because we're going to have company."

Jake stood up and held out his arm to his daughter. She paused and then came over to him. Dropping an arm over her shoulder, he gave her a quick hug. "I don't think Pete and Ben consider Lucy and Gianna their company. They might play with them for a little while, but mostly they are your company. The girls will want to do things with you."

"And what about Elizabeth? Is she your company?"

Jake froze, unsure how to answer. At once he was concerned about Molly's question as well as the unfamiliar tone of her voice. "I don't know. She's bringing her daughters over to play with you. I doubt Elizabeth will want to play with the boys, so I suppose she is."

"Then maybe you should put on a better shirt."

He looked down at his T-shirt. It was one of his favorites. "What's wrong with what I have on?"

"It's old and ratty. You wear it all the time. You should wear the shirt that Aunt Bethany got you for Christmas."

That shirt was made out of wool. "It's too hot for that."

"Then I'll find something better," she said. "You want to make a good impression on your company, don't you?"

Yes. And he'd thought he had accomplished that with this shirt. Obviously he'd been mistaken. Before he could reply, Molly dashed from the room. He pictured her rummaging through his closet, trying to find something she deemed appropriate for today, and he ran to catch up with her. The last thing he wanted was for her to grab a shirt and tie. Not that he was opposed to dressing up if the occasion called for it. Back when Maggie had been alive, he'd taken her to fancy five-star restaurants where a suit had been required. There was no way he was wearing anything approaching formal today. He didn't want Elizabeth to think he'd dressed up for her and get the wrong idea.

When Jake stepped into his room, Molly was reaching inside his closet. A second later, she pulled out two hangers and held them on either side of her so he could get a good look at them. She was smiling from ear to ear, clearly pleased with her choices. One—a dress shirt—was an instant no.

"Not the white one. It needs a tie, and I'm not going to wear a tie to a cookout. Besides, it's white. I don't want to get sauce on it."

Molly nodded. "That's true. I really like that shirt. I don't want it to get messed up."

"I like it too. You and your brothers gave it to me for Father's Day."

Molly shoved it back into the closet and then held out the other shirt to him. Not casual enough for a Saturday around the house. Especially since he expected to spend time standing over the grill.

"That's also a good shirt," he said.

"But you don't want to wear it."

He heard the disappointment in her voice, and his heart ached for her. He didn't want to dampen her enthusiasm. But he also had no intention of wearing that shirt.

"I think a T-shirt or even a pullover would be better for a casual afternoon at home. How about you help me choose one of those?"

"You'll wear the T-shirt I choose?"

He nodded. "Yes."

Molly smiled. "I can do that."

She opened the drawer and picked through the stack of shirts. After a moment, she pulled out an orange, yellow, and lime-green shirt that Jake had forgotten he had. A friend's son had been working as a salesclerk in a designer shop several summers ago. Wanting to support him, Jake had let the young man sell him an overpriced T-shirt. This one had been the least colorful of the selections. He'd bought it and immediately shoved it into the back of the drawer where it had remained for the past four years.

Until today. Well, there was no helping it. He'd told Molly that he would wear the T-shirt she chose.

"Thank you," he said.

Molly nodded and skipped from the room, closing the door behind her. When Jake was alone, he heaved a sigh and then pulled on the blindingly bright T-shirt. He looked in the mirror and winced. It looked even gaudier on. Luckily it was a sunny day, so he'd be wearing sunglasses.

Although he hadn't given his appearance more than a passing thought before Molly had started in on him, he suddenly felt self-conscious. He didn't want Elizabeth to think he normally wore tacky shirts like this.

Laughing at his foolishness, Jake went back downstairs. Ben and Pete were out back, chasing each other around the spacious yard and making enough noise for four kids. Jake wouldn't have it any other way. He loved the sound of their laughter. No matter how rough a day he'd had, knowing his kids were happy never failed to lift his spirits.

Jake was stepping into the front room when he heard a vehicle approaching. Despite telling himself this wasn't a date, his heart skipped a beat in anticipation. It made no sense to pretend he didn't find Elizabeth attractive. She was objectively gorgeous. More than just being blessed with good genes, she possessed a beautiful spirit. He liked the way she interacted with his kids, treating them with kindness and patience. Molly hadn't stopped talking about Elizabeth all week. No matter the topic of discussion, she'd managed to bring the woman into the conversation. In all fairness, she'd also mentioned Gianna and Lucy quite frequently, but her comments about Elizabeth stood out in his mind.

"They're here," Ben said, charging into the room. Jake had expected Molly to be excited, but he was a bit surprised to see that Ben was too. His kids had had friends come over to play, but they never got excited about their siblings' friends.

"Let's go say hello," Jake said. But he was talking to himself. Ben had already dashed outside.

Trying to slow his suddenly racing heartbeat, Jake stepped onto the porch. Elizabeth and her daughters were standing beside a black vehicle. Lucy and Gianna were laughing and talking with his kids. Apparently whatever shyness Lucy had felt around the boys before had vanished. Now the five kids were completely at ease with each other.

"We have swings and a tree house in the backyard," Pete said. "Come on—we'll show them to you."

The kids ran away, not giving him or Elizabeth a second glance.

"Well," Elizabeth said. "Talk about being forgotten. I guess I'm totally unnecessary now."

He laughed and descended the stairs. "Not to me. Welcome."

"Thanks."

"What do you have there?"

"The girls and I baked some bis—cookies for everyone."

Her miscue was a clear indicator that she was straddling two worlds. She had one foot in Australia and one in the States.

His life was so full right now that even if Elizabeth decided to stay in the States, he wouldn't have the time to properly date her. From the look of things, her life was just as busy as his. Two kids could take up just as much time and energy as three. She also had the added disadvantage of being in a place that was foreign to her kids.

"You didn't have to do that," he said.

"We were happy to do it. The girls and I enjoy baking

together. Besides, they were practically bouncing off the walls this morning in their eagerness to get here," she said. "This was a good way to fill the time."

"Molly was the same way today. Actually she's been excited all week."

"I'm so glad to hear that. My girls miss Australia and their pals. Making new friends will help them feel more at home."

He held out an arm, directing her to proceed him up the stairs and into the house. As she passed by, he inhaled and was treated to a whiff of her sweet scent. Her perfume was light with a hint of flowers. It suited her perfectly.

His eyes drifted down to her round bottom as she walked up the stairs. She was sexy without trying. Dressed in denim cutoffs that revealed her toned thighs and a yellow T-shirt with pink flowers on the front, she was a ray of sunshine. Distracted by the gentle sway of her hips, he missed a step and nearly fell. He grabbed the banister in the nick of time.

Elizabeth glanced over her shoulder, a mischievous grin on her face. "Still trying to get the hang of walking and talking at the same time?"

Laughter burst from him. "I've just about mastered it. It's remembering which leg to use first that has me confused."

She laughed and tossed her head, sending her curls cascading down her back. The dark tresses looked so soft that his fingers ached to touch them. Instead, he opened the screen door for her.

Elizabeth stepped inside and looked around. "You have a nice house."

"Thanks. It has its idiosyncrasies as many old houses do, but I love every creaking floor and slightly drafty room."

"It has character."

"That it does. Sometimes a little too much." He led her

through the house and into the kitchen. She set her container of cookies on the table and then turned back to look at him. Every cell of her body exuded joy. And sex appeal. For a moment he was hypnotized by her radiance and couldn't move.

When he realized he was staring, he gave himself a mental shake. He was a grown man, not some lovestruck teen. So why was he gawking like he'd never seen a woman before, much less been alone with one? "Would you like a drink?"

"No. I'm fine."

"Then let's go outside where we can keep an eye on the kids. The weather's perfect for sitting on the patio."

"That sounds good to me," Elizabeth said as they went outside.

Jake and Maggie had planted several flower beds when they'd moved in, and he'd done everything in his power to maintain them. He kept the same flowers that Maggie had selected in the very same arrangement. The blooms weren't as glorious as when Maggie had been in charge, but he did his best.

"This is beautiful," Elizabeth said. "You must be one of the lucky ones who's been blessed with a green thumb."

"I don't know about that. What you see is the result of years of practice. Do you garden?"

"No. I learned long ago that I don't have what it takes to keep plants alive. Either I overwater or forget to water altogether. Years of practice won't change that," she said ruefully. "But I appreciate beautiful gardens. Yours is a work of art."

"Maggie studied landscape architecture," Jake explained. "She was good at finding the right combination of flowers."

"She was clearly quite gifted."

He nodded. He'd been so proud of his wife. For a reason

unknown to him, he was glad that Elizabeth didn't possess Maggie's green thumb. The last thing he wanted was a poor imitation of his wife. Not only that, he was intrigued by the qualities that made Elizabeth different. He wanted to learn more about what made her tick.

"Can you tell me more about Maggie?" Elizabeth asked. "Unless that's none of my business."

She was direct. He liked that. "I don't mind talking about Maggie. At least not now. After she died, just thinking about her was painful enough to make my heart stop beating so talking about her was out of the question."

"I know what you mean."

Yes, she did. "Maggie was kind. And smart. I knew her from the time I was five, so I can't claim it was love at first sight. But once I knew what love was, I knew she was the one and that we would get married." He sighed. "Maggie loved being a wife and mother and making a home for all of us. She was happiest when we were all snuggled together on the couch watching a movie."

"How did she die?" Elizabeth's voice was soft, but he still heard the sadness in her words. Only a person who'd lost a beloved spouse could relate to the depth of pain he felt.

"Giving birth to Ben."

She gasped. "No. I'm so sorry."

"It was sudden. Everything was going fine, then Maggie began to hemorrhage." Jake sucked in a ragged breath. Even after all this time he was incapable of telling the story in a detached, unemotional manner. "They couldn't stop the bleeding. And just like that, what started out as one of the best days of my life turned into a nightmare. I couldn't celebrate my son's birth because I was mourning the loss of my wife. God forgive me…for one horrible moment, I—I actually blamed Ben for Maggie's death."

"Obviously, I never met your wife and would never dream of speaking for her. But as a mother, I would give up my life for my daughters in a heartbeat."

He nodded. "I would do the same for my children. It was just so hard to accept that I'd lost the woman I loved more than everything in the world."

Elizabeth glanced over at Ben. He and Pete were chasing the girls around the yard, pretending to be monsters. Then as one, the girls stopped and turned the tables on Ben and Pete and began chasing them. No doubt they would all sleep well tonight.

"Ben seems like a happy child."

"He is. Of the three, he's the most easy-going. He rarely puts up a fuss and doesn't mind when the older kids boss him around. But then, as the youngest, there probably isn't much he can do about that, so he may as well roll with the punches."

Elizabeth laughed, and his stomach lurched. Even the most minor things about her aroused him. That wasn't good.

"Can you tell me about your husband?" he asked.

The light in her eyes dimmed as she sobered. "Arlo was the best man—the best person—I ever met. He never had a bad word to say about anyone, and nobody had anything negative to say about him. He was big and gregarious. The life of the party. People naturally gravitated to him. He was a rodeo star, but he never acted like a celebrity. He was down to earth. He absolutely loved our girls. He was the best father they could have had. The best husband I could have dreamed of. One minute we were making chicken parmigiana for dinner. The next he was gone. Dead from a heart attack. He had an undiagnosed heart condition. Now all we have is memories. The girls were so little when he died, they don't even have those."

Although she'd spoken matter-of-factly, Jake heard the misery in her voice, and his heart ached in sympathy. "Losing the person that you love sucks, doesn't it?"

"Yes. It took a lot for me not to be bitter. Arlo was such a good man. I loved him so much. We all did. There are so many bad people in the world doing all manner of evil, and they're still alive when he isn't. Why was he the one who had to die? How is that fair?"

"The simple answer is that it isn't fair. Nothing in life is."

"I know. It would be great if it was. But…" She sighed. "Most of the time I accept the randomness of it all. I have to. I have two little girls who are taking their cues from me. I don't want them to be bitter, so I don't have a choice but to accept it. That's the only way to heal my heart."

"And has it healed?"

Before she could answer, the kids ran over and opened the back door.

"Where are you going?" Jake asked.

"Inside. Lucy and Gianna want to see our rooms," Molly said.

"Your room, or Ben and Pete's room?" Jake asked.

"Both of them," Pete said.

"Your room is dirty," he pointed out.

"So what? We don't care," Pete said.

"So do you care if Elizabeth sees your room?" Jake asked. "Nope."

"Mine too," Molly told him. "*My* room is clean."

Jake turned to Elizabeth. "Would you like to see the rest of the house?"

"I'd love to." She winked at Pete, who smiled broadly. "Even the messy room."

Jake and Elizabeth waited until the kids came barreling back into the yard before getting up and making a detour to the kitchen. They poured glasses of lemonade for the kids and got them settled around the patio table with cut fruit before heading up the back stairs.

When they reached the second floor, Jake turned to Elizabeth. "Fair warning, the boys' room isn't just dirty. It's this side of a disaster area."

She chuckled. "I'm sure I've seen worse."

"I don't know about that," he said.

"You have to know how to pick your battles."

"A clean room isn't a hill I'm willing to die on." Pete and Ben's room was the first room they came upon. He stopped at the open and she peered inside.

She gave him a pained smile and patted his arm. "You have my sympathy."

"Thanks," he said dryly.

Molly's door was open, and they glanced inside it. He'd painted the room a pale green last year and bought her a white comforter with pink-and-green flowers. Molly was really proud of the way it looked. Her room was always spotless.

"This is so pretty," Elizabeth said.

"She loves it."

"How many bedrooms do you have?"

"Six. Maggie and I wanted to have a big family and we figured there would be less chaos if the kids had their own rooms."

"But Pete and Ben share."

"That's the way they want it. Ben is our traveling kid. Maggie and I prepared a nursery for him before he was born. He slept in there for maybe a week before I moved his crib into my bedroom. I needed to have him close to me. I couldn't rest if he wasn't. Losing Maggie made me afraid of everything. I got it in my head that Ben would die too. It didn't make sense, but it was my reality." Jake wasn't ordinarily this open about his feelings, especially with some-one he just met, but there was something about Elizabeth that made sharing easy. He felt comfortable around her, as if they had been friends for a long time.

"Fear is often irrational," Elizabeth said. "Especially when coupled with grief."

"When Ben turned one, Molly wanted him to sleep in her room. To her, he was a living doll and she loved play-ing with him. So, I put the crib in there, and that's where he stayed for a while," Jake explained. "When Pete started school, he discovered that some of the other boys shared rooms with their brothers, and he wanted to do the same. So I moved Ben's bed in there. They've been together ever since. Poor kid has never had a room of his own."

"Maybe not, but he must enjoy being in demand."

Jake chuckled. "I suppose. To him it's perfectly normal. But if he ever wants his own room or Pete decides to kick him out—whichever comes first—there are plenty of empty rooms for him to choose from."

They continued down the corridor, pausing to look at the framed photos of the kids hanging on the walls. Jake opened three more doors revealing a guest room, although they rarely had overnight guests, and two rooms he used for storage. Then he reached his closed bedroom door. He hesitated. No woman other than Maggie had been in this room. Was he re-ally going to allow Elizabeth into his personal space?

"Can't remember if you made your bed or left dirty clothes scattered around?" Elizabeth joked.

Her words made him laugh and removed all reluctance to allow her into his room. She wasn't looking to make a place for herself in his home. To her, this was one more stop on the tour.

"Unlike Pete and Ben, I always make up my bed. And my clothes are in the hamper."

"No stray socks lying around?"

"Not in here." He swung open the door and stood aside so she could go in. Ridiculously, his heart paused as he waited for her reaction. He'd tried to keep things the same as they'd been when Maggie had shared the room with him, but that hadn't been possible. Time had taken its toll on the furniture as well as the linen. Three years ago, he'd painted the walls and bought new furniture and bedding. He'd gone with oak furniture, cream walls, and navy curtains and linen. It was basic, but it suited his needs. Now he wondered if he should have taken his sister up on her offer to help him decorate with a bit more style.

"Nice," Elizabeth said.

"Do you really think that, or are you just being polite?"

"I mean it. It suits you."

Exchanging smiles, they left the room and went back downstairs. The kids had finished with their snacks and were playing on the swings.

Jake started a fire in the grill.

"Do you need any help with the food?" Elizabeth asked.

"I never say no to a hand."

She held up both of hers. "I've got two. Take your pick."

Chapter Five

There was something so nice about working side by side with Jake to get a meal on the table, being part of a team doing whatever it took to accomplish a goal. They moved in tandem as if they'd been cooking together for years. Elizabeth had gotten used to doing household tasks alone, but now she realized how much she enjoyed having a partner. Cooking with Jake was comfortable—perhaps too comfortable— and she felt a hint of guilt that she brushed aside. She wasn't going to allow misplaced guilt to ruin today.

They reached for the cheese at the same time, and their hands brushed. Elizabeth's skin immediately warmed at the contact, and she felt a seed of desire sprout inside her. Their eyes met, and attraction blossomed between them.

Then Jake blinked and stepped away. "I'll go check on the grill."

Before she could think of a reply he was gone. Elizabeth blew out a breath. She didn't need this ridiculous attraction to complicate her life further. She gave herself a stern talking-to before joining everyone outside.

Elizabeth couldn't resist eyeing Jake while he manned the grill. Dressed in a bright T-shirt that had to be either a Father's Day gift or the result of a lost bet and faded jeans that emphasized his muscular thighs, he looked good enough to make her mouth water. Her heart thumped loudly at the sight of him. He was so attractive she couldn't stop sneaking glances at him.

And that was a problem. She knew that physical attraction was something that couldn't be controlled, yet she still felt as if she was being unfaithful to Arlo. Even knowing that Arlo wouldn't want her to spend the rest of her life alone wasn't enough to shake that feeling. But somehow she would.

"Is dinner ready?" Pete asked, running over. The other kids were behind him, expectant expressions on their faces.

"Yes," Jake said. "So everyone go wash your hands."

"My hands aren't dirty," Pete said, holding his palms out for Jake to see.

"You're kidding, right?"

"No." He pulled out a chair and sat down.

Jake looked at his son. "Go wash your hands."

"Come on, Pete," Molly said. "We're hungry. And your hands have germs. You just can't see them."

There was plenty of dirt that Elizabeth *could* see.

Pete frowned, but he followed the rest of the kids inside.

"What is it with boys and soap?" Elizabeth asked.

"I have no idea. I suppose we just like to rough it."

She laughed. "Is that what they're calling it these days?"

"That's the best I can come up with on such short notice."

Jake placed the platter of burgers and hot dogs on the table while Elizabeth brought out the side dishes. She was filling the last glass with lemonade when the kids came bounding back. Gianna and Lucy walked over to her and held out their hands for her inspection. She nodded and smiled. "Good job, girls."

Ben watched them for a minute. Then he shrugged, walked over to Elizabeth, and held out his hands. She inspected them and then smiled. "Good job, Ben. You're ready to eat."

He grinned, then sat down between the twins. There was a lot of talking as Elizabeth and Jake filled everyone's plate with their requested food. Once everyone had their food, Jake's kids picked up their burgers or hot dogs.

"They didn't pray," Gianna said to Elizabeth. She looked around the table. "Don't you pray before you eat?"

"Nope. We just eat," Pete said. He took another bite out of his burger.

"Are we going to pray, Mum?" Lucy asked, looking at Elizabeth.

Elizabeth raised her children to express gratitude before each meal. Clearly Jake wasn't rearing his children in the same way. Before she could reply, Jake answered.

"Of course," he said. He looked at Pete. "Stop eating so we can say grace."

Pete heaved a heavy sigh, but he dropped his burger onto his plate and bowed his head. Gianna, Lucy, and Elizabeth recited the prayer that she'd taught them from a young age. Once they were done, Gianna smiled and picked up her hot dog.

"We used to pray with Mommy," Molly said. "But we don't anymore."

"I don't remember that," Pete said slowly.

"Me neither," Ben added.

Elizabeth glanced over at Jake, who appeared pained. Wordlessly, he picked up his burger and took a big bite.

Deciding that Jake needed a moment alone with his thoughts and a change of subject, she tasted her burger. "This is delicious. You are definitely the grill master."

He gave her a smile, clearly grateful to talk about something else.

Once they'd taken a few bites and satisfied their initial hunger, the kids began to recount the activities of the day, talking over each other in their zeal. It became clear that the five of them had had lots of fun together. What was surprising was how well her girls had gotten along with the boys.

Jake didn't talk much during the meal, and Elizabeth wondered if he was okay. They'd discussed some pretty heavy topics earlier, stirring up some strong emotions. Hearing his sons say they didn't remember something about Maggie had to cut deep.

Once they'd finished their meal, Elizabeth said, "I guess the girls and I should get going."

"Already?" Molly asked.

"But we just got here," Gianna said.

"Yeah, they just got here," Ben added.

As one, the other kids began to beg to keep playing, explaining at great length and with loud volume the game they hadn't finished—the game they needed to finish.

Jake glanced at Elizabeth. She shrugged. It was up to him. She didn't have any other plans for the rest of the day and was content to stay awhile longer. As he'd pointed out earlier, the weather was perfect for sitting outside. But Elizabeth didn't want to overstay her welcome.

"How about we let you guys play for thirty more minutes," Jake said, picking up Ben and swinging him onto his massive shoulders. "Will that work for you?"

"Yes!" Ben exclaimed. He clapped his hands, clearly delighted to be on his father's shoulders.

"Can you pick me up too?" Gianna asked, patting Jake on his thigh.

"And me?" Lucy added. "That looks like fun."

"Sure he can," Ben answered before his father could. "Dad picks us up like this all the time."

Elizabeth's heart squeezed with pain at Ben's casual words. Lucy and Gianna no longer had a father to carry them on his shoulders. Arlo used to carry them both at once, holding one giggling twin on each shoulder. They'd absolutely loved it. Thankfully Elizabeth had pictures of the three of them with wide smiles on their faces.

Jake lowered Ben, setting him on his feet, then looked at the twins. "Who is first?"

"Gianna, since she asked first," Lucy said.

Gianna giggled in anticipation and raised her arms. When Jake swung her over his head and set her onto his shoulders, she laughed loudly. Her smile was wide and bright enough to send Elizabeth's spirits soaring.

"Look at me, Mummy. I'm big."

"I see."

Jake walked around the yard, taking loping strides much to Gianna's delight. When he returned, he stooped down and lowered her onto the ground.

"Your turn," Gianna said, looking at Lucy.

"I don't want you to run with me," Lucy said, holding out her arms in front of her, preventing Jake from picking her up.

"I won't go any faster than you want me to," he said.

"Do you promise?"

"Cross my heart," he said, using a finger to make a cross on his chest.

"Okay." Lucy stepped up to him, trust written all over her face.

Jake lifted her carefully and settled her on his shoulders. He walked around the yard taking slow steps.

"You can go faster," Lucy said.

He sped up and then glanced at her.

"Faster," she ordered, and after a second repeated, "Faster!"

Laughing, Jake loped around the yard at the same speed as he'd taken Gianna. Apparently Lucy wasn't afraid after all. Quite the opposite—she was having the time of her life. When the ride ended, Jake set her on the ground.

"Thank you," Lucy said, a wide grin on her face.

"My pleasure."

"Now you can start our thirty minutes," Molly said.

"How do you figure that?" Jake asked.

"Because you were playing with them. We couldn't finish our game. Now we can."

"I suppose you're right."

The kids raced over to the tree house and swings while Jake walked back over to the patio, his long-legged stride casual. It seemed to Elizabeth he was completely oblivious to how attractive he was. Of course, with three kids to raise on his own and no desire for a relationship, he probably didn't give his appeal a second thought.

So why was she so focused on it?

"Thanks for giving my girls pony rides."

He slid into the chair beside her. "You're welcome."

"I do what I can, including giving them pony rides, but there are some things only a man can do."

"I completely understand. I know my kids are missing a woman's touch. My sister, Bethany, helps out when she can, but she's an aunt. That's a totally different role."

"Molly told me about her. She's a wedding singer, right?"

He nodded. "Yes. And quite a gifted one. But then, I'm biased."

She grinned. "And you should be. Do you sing?"

He shook his head. "Not even in the shower. Trust me when I say that Bethany got all of the musical talent in our family."

"So I can't expect to be serenaded in the future."

The words popped out of her mouth before she could stop them. Hopefully he knew that she'd been joking. The last thing she wanted was for him to think that she was coming on to him. Was she coming on to him unconsciously?

He laughed. "No. Sorry. You'll have to stick to the radio."

She relaxed, relieved that he could tell she'd been kidding. Leaning back in her chair, she sighed. "This has been great. I can't remember the last time I had this much fun."

He looked into her eyes. His were bright. Sincere. "Neither can I. So why are you in such a hurry to leave?"

"I'm not. You seemed a bit distracted while we were eating. I figured you were ready to get things back to normal around here. Maybe lower the volume a bit."

He chuckled. The sound reached inside her, making her heart go pitter-patter. He picked up his lemonade and downed it, then swirled the ice in the glass. "When you reach a certain number of kids, the noise level doesn't matter. Three kids or five, it's going to be loud. Especially when two of them are boys."

"I'll have to take your word for it." She smiled. "But one thing I have noticed is my girls are a lot more rambunctious today than they've been in a long time."

"Is that good or bad?"

"It's definitely good. They became a lot quieter after Arlo died, and they clung to each other. Their tight bond became even tighter."

"And that's bad?" Jake asked.

"In their case, yes." Elizabeth sighed. "They began to exclude other people. After a while, they rebounded, becoming more like themselves. Still… I often wonder if losing their father changed their personalities permanently."

"I believe not having a mother definitely changed my kids. Especially Molly. As a man, I can't teach her how to be a woman. The older she gets, the less I understand her. I have a feeling her teenage years will be even more challenging. Not to mention that she's taken on the role of mother to her brothers. I've told her repeatedly that she's not responsible for raising them, but it's like talking to a wall. I don't push her too hard because being a big sister is important to her."

Elizabeth frowned. "It's all so hard. I spend way too much time questioning myself and wondering if I'm making mistakes with the girls."

"Take it from me," he said. "Once you make a decision, stop debating it. Just stick with it. At least until you have proof that you're going in the wrong direction. Then turn around and start again."

"Is that what you do?"

"It's what I *try* to do. Sometimes I'm more successful than others. But practice makes perfect, and all that."

Elizabeth nodded. She liked his honesty and the way he didn't act as if he had it all together. He was muddling through, the same as she was.

By unspoken agreement, they turned the conversation to inconsequential matters. It was good to set aside the challenges of single-parenthood and talk about places to eat when she doesn't feel like cooking.

"DJ's Deluxe is hands down the best place to get ribs," Jake said. "You might not want to take the kids, though."

"If I want to eat out with the twins, what do you recommend?"

"Bronco Brick Oven Pizza. Or Pastabilities."

"Do you go there a lot?"

"Not really. But it's a nice change from my cooking. Of course, my mom is a great cook. My parents live in Bronco

Valley and they have us over for dinner quite often." He grinned. "Nothing beats my mom's pot roast."

Time flew by, and those thirty minutes stretched into forty-five and then an hour. Jake gave the kids a five-minute warning so they could wrap up their game.

"Will Molly be free at any time next week?" Elizabeth asked. "She was quite a big help with the girls."

"She's free every day."

Once they decided on Tuesday and Thursday, Jake said, "Thank you again for doing this."

"There's no need for thanks. Molly is the one helping me."

"You're helping her too. She couldn't stop talking about how much fun she had. She wasn't only talking about Gianna and Lucy. She talked about you nonstop. Being around you is good for her."

"It was mutually beneficial."

He covered her hand with his. Once again electricity shot throughout her body. Their eyes met. Held. Elizabeth struggled to slow her racing heart. The blood pulsed in her veins and she couldn't look away to save her life.

Jake leaned closer and Elizabeth felt herself edging closer to him. They moved slowly as if pulled by a force neither of them could control. Then Jake blinked and jerked away. Realizing where she was, Elizabeth did the same.

Molly ran over then, the rest of the kids behind her. "We know our five minutes is up, so we decided to come before you called us again."

Jake stood and placed an affectionate hand on his daughter's shoulder. "Thank you for being so mature and cooperating with us."

Elizabeth inhaled deeply trying to slow her suddenly racing heart. She felt moisture on her forehead and swiped at it before anyone could see. It took a long moment, but she managed to regain control of her emotions. She stood.

"Can we come back again?" Lucy asked.

"Yes. You're welcome anytime." Jake turned from Lucy and looked directly at Elizabeth. "All of you."

Elizabeth's knees wobbled.

There were lots of hugs as the kids said goodbye. Once Gianna and Lucy were buckled into their booster seats, Elizabeth turned on the SUV. Before she drove away, she glanced at Jake and his children, feeling as if her life had just changed.

She wished she could be assured that change was a good thing.

Jake watched as Elizabeth drove away, wondering why he suddenly felt as if he'd just lost an important person in his life. This bereft feeling didn't make sense. Elizabeth was barely in his life. They weren't a couple. They were only friends. He rubbed his chin. Could you count someone as a friend after only knowing them for a short time? He didn't know if there was a time requirement, but he felt that he and Elizabeth were friends. They were connected on such an elemental level that their relationship had even more depth.

He and Maggie had had a way of communicating that hadn't required words. They'd understood each other's moods and expressions. Their connection had been solid. He'd missed knowing someone completely, missed being known completely. Now he felt that same type of connection with Elizabeth. He didn't know how to feel about that. On one hand it felt like betrayal. On the other it felt right. Maggie wouldn't want him to mourn her loss forever. She'd been generous and loving. There was no doubt she would want him to have a happy life even if she couldn't be a part of it.

Intellectually he'd always known that. Since he hadn't been attracted to anyone before Elizabeth, he hadn't been forced to confront that reality. Or his feelings. Now, presented with the possibility of opening his heart to someone, he was confused and cautious.

"That was fun," Ben said, grabbing Jake by the hand and then swinging their joined hands. "I like Lucy and Gianna."

"Do you?"

He nodded. "Do you want to know why?"

"If you want to tell me."

"I like not being the youngest. I'm six, and they're only five. That makes me one of the big kids."

"Does it?"

"Yep." Ben gave their hands one last swing before letting go of Jake's and running across the yard. He hopped on the swing and immediately began swinging high, singing a song as he sailed through the air.

His children's easy acceptance of Gianna and Lucy was a good thing. If he and Elizabeth decided to pursue a relationship in the future, that was one problem they wouldn't have to deal with. Blending families was never easy. The thought alone made Jake's stomach pitch, and he ordered himself to slow down. He wasn't ready for a commitment. From what he could see, neither was Elizabeth. So why was the thought of getting closer to her so appealing?

Jake sat down and watched his kids play. He'd spent many evenings in this very chair over the years, feeling perfectly content. Now, though, he felt lonely. He'd enjoyed being with Elizabeth this afternoon—perhaps more than he should've. He missed her now—missed talking to her. The closeness of walking outside with her, of laughing with a partner. But, he remembered, she might be returning to Australia soon.

If that wasn't a warning that he needed to keep his distance, he didn't know what was.

Chapter Six

"I really like the way you combed Gianna's and Lucy's hair," Molly said the following Tuesday. The girls were in their room gathering books for Molly to read to them. Elizabeth had brought several of their favorite books from Australia, but she'd read them so many times that even she was tired of them. So she'd bought a dozen new books for them yesterday. Elizabeth had planned to read one new book a night, but the minute Molly had stepped into the house, the girls had asked her to read some of them. When she'd agreed, they'd raced away to get their new treasures.

"Thank you."

"Do you think that you can do my hair the way you did theirs?"

"Then she will look just like us," Gianna said, returning to the room with a book in each hand.

"We could even be sisters," Lucy added, stepping beside Gianna. She was also holding two books. Apparently they intended Molly to read for quite a while.

"I can definitely braid your hair, but it won't look exactly like theirs," Elizabeth warned. She'd braided the front of her daughters' hair in neat cornrows that she'd pulled into two Afro puffs. Colorful barrettes and beads completed the style. "Your hair is a different texture. It won't puff up like theirs."

"But you can still braid the front?" Molly asked hopefully.

"Absolutely."

Elizabeth grabbed the comb, brush, and barrettes and then directed Molly to sit on the floor in front of her. Gianna and Lucy grabbed new coloring books and crayons from the table and sat nearby. Elizabeth parted Molly's hair down the middle and secured one section in a scrunchie.

Molly chatted happily as Elizabeth sectioned her hair and began to braid. "This is going to be so cool. I like different styles, but I don't know how to do any of them. Sometimes I wear a headband or put it in a scrunchie, but mostly I just wear it straight down."

"It can be hard to learn on your own. You do a good job, though. Your hair always looks nice."

As kids, Elizabeth, her sisters, and cousins had spent hours styling each other's hair. Many of them had been adopted and were of different races and ethnicities. Faith and Elizabeth were Black, Tori and Amy were white, and Carly was Latina, so they'd become experts at doing hair of different textures and lengths. Although Elizabeth and her relatives didn't resemble each other physically, their love for each other made it clear that they were family.

After she finished the braids, Elizabeth gathered Molly's hair into two ponytails. Her hair was straight, so there was no way Elizabeth could pull it into puffs. After a moment, she had an idea. She rolled Molly's hair into two buns and then added barrettes. They weren't exactly Afro puffs, but they looked good.

Elizabeth grabbed a hand mirror and gave it to Molly. "What do you think?"

Molly stared at her reflection, turning from one side to the other. Her smile grew wider with each passing second.

Still holding the mirror, she reached out and hugged Elizabeth tightly. "I love it. Thank you so much."

"You're welcome." She returned Molly's embrace. Now she saw firsthand what Molly was missing by not having a mother around to teach her how to style her hair, about fashion, or a hundred other little things, and it broke her heart. Elizabeth could only imagine how Molly would feel attending mother-and-daughter events in the future. Would she choose to skip them altogether, or would she ask Jake's sister to accompany her? Perhaps Jake would be involved with a woman by then. Elizabeth felt a twinge of jealousy at that thought, although she had no right to feel that way.

"Do you guys like it?" Molly asked, turning to Lucy and Gianna.

"Yes. You could be twins with us," Lucy said.

"We used to be two twins, but now we're three twins," Gianna said.

Molly laughed. "There's no such thing as three twins. Three kids who look alike are called triplets. So that's what we are. We're triplets—aren't we, Elizabeth?"

Elizabeth smiled. "I suppose it would be all right if you called yourselves that."

"Can you polish my nails like theirs?" Molly asked.

Elizabeth and her daughters had weekly home spa days. Gianna and Lucy used to protest when it was time to get their nails trimmed. Once Elizabeth had begun giving them mani-pedis, that had all changed. Now they looked forward to having their nails filed and polished. Yesterday she'd polished their nails in spring colors—white, yellow, and three shades of green. She'd then used those same colors to paint sunflowers on two nails on each hand.

She smiled. There was still lots of polish left. And Molly

looked so hopeful there was no way Elizabeth would re-
fuse. "Of course."

"Yay." Molly hugged herself with glee. Gianna and Lucy
joined hands and jumped up and down, celebrating with
their friend.

"I'll go grab everything. While I do that, I need you to
wash your hands."

Molly raced to the bathroom, and Gianna and Lucy followed right behind her. A minute later, they were back.
The girls clustered around the coffee table in the small
living room.

Elizabeth trimmed Molly's nails so that they were all
the same length and then filed them into neat ovals. "Do
you like the way I shaped them?"

Molly nodded, a wide smile on her face. She hadn't
stopped grinning since Elizabeth had styled her hair. No
doubt, she would fall asleep smiling.

As Elizabeth worked, Molly talked happily about life on
the ranch. She spoke about her brothers, confirming Jake's
statement that Molly was definitely a mother hen. She also
expressed a desire to wear more trendy clothes.

"But Daddy doesn't know what they are. He doesn't know
anything about clothes." She looked at her plain T-shirt and
frowned. "Neither do I."

Elizabeth empathized with the girl even as she sympathized with Jake. It couldn't be easy for either of them.
Elizabeth was lucky to be raising girls. She would be out to
sea if she was raising a boy on her own. She could offer to
help, but she didn't want Jake to think she was auditioning
for the role of woman in his life. Besides, he'd mentioned
that he had a sister. If he wanted, he could always turn to
her for advice.

"I like your clothes," Gianna said loyally. "I think you look pretty."

"So do I," Lucy said. "You look really pretty."

"Thank you," Molly said.

Lucy and Gianna leaned close, watching and assisting as Elizabeth worked. With each finger she polished, they complimented her on her work.

"Now we just need to wait until the polish dries so I can paint on the flowers."

"How long will that take?" Molly asked. She was holding her fingers straight, being careful not to touch one to the other.

"About ten minutes or so."

"We usually sing while we wait," Lucy said, launching into the alphabet song. Gianna joined in when Lucy reached *E*. They sang the song three times before they tired of it. From there, they began to sing the kookaburra song, the Australian nursery rhyme Elizabeth had been singing to them since before they could walk.

Molly smiled when they finished. "That was very good. I would clap, but I don't want to mess up my nails."

"That's very smart of you," Elizabeth said. "I think we're ready for the flowers."

Molly squirmed excitedly.

Elizabeth worked freehand but managed to make the flowers look identical to the ones she'd painted onto the twins' nails.

"Now you need to sit very still and be careful with your fingers," Gianna advised Molly.

"We'll turn on the telly so we can watch something. And we'll remind you not to move your hands," Lucy said. She grabbed the remote and turned on one of their favorite Disney movies. It was in the middle of the program, but that didn't seem to matter to them.

"Do you like this?" Gianna asked. "It's not a baby show."

"I do like it. This is my favorite princess movie."

"Ours too," Lucy and Gianna chimed in together.

The girls sat next to each other on the floor, leaning against the back of the sofa as they watched the movie. Lucy and Gianna had seen it so often that they knew every word of dialogue. When the female lead broke into song, they joined in, singing with gusto. Molly looked at them and after hesitating briefly, she joined in. Her voice started out tentatively. Self-conscious. After singing a few of the lyrics, she sang louder and with confidence. Eventually all three of them were singing at the top of their lungs.

Elizabeth was glad to see it even if her ears would have been happier with a lower volume. She knew there came a point when children—especially girls—began to concern themselves with their peers' opinions of them. It was inevitable. She was happy that Molly still felt the freedom to be herself and could enjoy childish pleasures for a while longer.

Elizabeth turned her attention from the girls and went to work. The Pony Club had been a hit with parents and kids alike, and Rylee had contacted Elizabeth about holding a second session. Since the girls were occupied, it was the perfect time to reach out to Rylee.

She grabbed her phone and punched in Rylee's number. "Is this a good time?"

"It's the best. Especially if you're calling to tell me you're going to run the club again."

Elizabeth laughed. "I am. I'm pleased that there was a lot of interest."

"That's putting it mildly. Not a day goes by when I don't

get at least one phone call from a parent asking if there will be a second event and wanting to sign up their children."

"I imagine sooner would be better than later. That way we can strike while the interest is high."

"Don't worry about that," Rylee said quickly. "I don't think interest will be waning anytime soon. As a matter of fact, would you be willing to hold it for three days? Or maybe even a week?"

Elizabeth thought a minute before answering. How would that affect her daughters? She knew the girls had enjoyed themselves last time. But they were having a good time with Molly now. Even so, it would do them good to be around other kids.

Now Elizabeth had Molly's well-being to consider as well. Molly enjoyed being a mother's helper. She'd told Elizabeth that she had big plans for the money she was earning, although she had not shared what those plans were. If camp was only three days, Molly could still work for Elizabeth the other two days. That was a win-win.

"I can commit to three days right now. I'll need to check out a few things to see if a week is doable," she said.

"That sounds fair," Rylee said. "How about we talk in a couple of days?"

"That works. But I'm not sure if Ross will be able to attend."

"Don't worry about that. There are a couple of other rodeo riders we can contact."

"I'll also ask my sisters and cousins. If they're in town, I'm sure I can convince someone to help." That was one thing Elizabeth knew about her family—they were always willing to share the joy of rodeo with children.

Elizabeth ended the call at the same time the movie ended. The girls cheered, and movie forgotten, they looked at Molly's nails. She tentatively touched the yellow-painted nail. "It's dry."

"I told you it would be," Elizabeth said.

"I can't wait until everyone sees how pretty my nails are. They're going to love them."

"They look as pretty as ours do," Gianna said, holding up her hands and admiring her nails.

"You should let Mummy do them all the time," Lucy said. "You should come to our spa day."

Molly looked at Elizabeth, curiosity shining in her eyes. "What's spa day?"

"That's when Mummy does our nails," Gianna said. "We have drinks with fruit in them."

"And umbrellas," Lucy added. "Not real ones. Little paper ones."

"And we watch *Bluey* while our nails dry," Gianna said.

"I like having cotton balls between my toes," Lucy said with a giggle. "It tickles."

"Mummy does her nails like ours."

Elizabeth held up her hands for Molly to see.

"Could I come?" Molly asked, hope in her voice.

"Of course. We'll ask your dad to bring you."

"And I can have a fancy drink?"

"Absolutely. That's part of the fun. And I'll give you a pedicure if you want one of those too."

Molly laughed. Then she looked at her feet. She was wearing well-worn cowboy boots. "I do. I can't wait. That is going to be so much fun."

"Then it's a plan. I'll talk to your father about it when he picks you up."

Just mentioning Jake made Elizabeth's heart skip a foolish beat. She frowned, disgusted with her lack of control. This ridiculous attraction to him was an unwanted distraction that was taking up more and more of her time. She had a decision to make and didn't need to expend mental energy on Jake like she had last night. She was still miffed at herself for having dreamed about him yet again. It was as if the universe was trying to replace Arlo in her heart, something that she would never permit.

Jake stood at the back of the classroom and watched as his boys went through their drills. He'd dropped Molly at Elizabeth's before karate class had started, but there hadn't been time for more than a quick hello before he'd needed to leave. The degree of disappointment he'd felt at not being able to have coffee and conversation with Elizabeth again was more than the situation warranted. They'd just seen each other over the weekend and talked for hours. But that didn't change his desire to be with her today.

"Pete and Ben are doing quite well in class."

Jake barely managed to suppress the annoyance at the sweetly cloying voice. He pasted on a polite smile as he turned to face Cindy. Her eight-year-old son, River, was also taking karate. Cindy had been divorced for several months, and she'd made numerous changes to her appearance. She'd bleached her hair and teeth and begun wearing tight clothes. She'd also made it plain that she was on the prowl for a replacement husband. To her, Jake fit the bill. She dropped hints about going out every time she saw him. He always deflected, but either she didn't get the message or she thought she could wear him down.

She wasn't the first woman who had believed that. Maggie hadn't been gone for two months before several women began making a play for him.

Back then, his pain had made him blunt. Time had dulled the pain, and he was more diplomatic now. He didn't want to hurt Cindy. Until she had gotten the ridiculous idea of blending their families into her head, Cindy had been a friend of his. He used to look forward to talking to her while their boys took their lesson. Now? Not so much.

"So is River," he said.

"I imagine that Pete and Ben practice with each other during the week."

Jake shook his head and laughed. "Not as much as you would think. They like class, but getting them to practice their kata takes a bit of nudging."

"River doesn't have anyone to practice with," Cindy said. "I was thinking that perhaps I could bring River out to the ranch and he could practice with Pete. They're the same age after all. Pete might prefer practicing with him instead of Ben. I could grab dinner at DJ's Deluxe for everyone and a bottle of wine for us. We could make a night of it."

"That sounds like a lot of driving just for a few minutes of practice."

Cindy opened her mouth as if to argue when one of the other mothers stepped up. She lived in town, and her son was a year older than Pete and River. An idea formed in Jake's mind. "Hey, Claire. Cindy is trying to find someone for River to practice with during the week. I live so far out, but you live in town. Maybe Daniel would like to practice with him."

Claire's eyes lit up. "Daniel would love to practice with River. Cindy, what time is good for you?"

Cindy glared at Jake, who managed to keep a self-satisfied expression from his face. He didn't want to hurt her feelings, but he wasn't interested in playing happy family with her. If she didn't get the message this time, he would be more direct in the future. He wasn't looking to add a woman to his life. *What about Elizabeth?*

That unexpected thought came from out of nowhere, and he did his best to shut it down. Elizabeth wasn't like Cindy or any of the others who'd tried to use his kids to get close to him. She wasn't trying to shove her way into his life.

And if she did try? What would he do?

The answer came quickly—he had no idea.

Class ended and not a moment too soon. After the boys changed into their street clothes, they all hopped into the SUV and Jake headed out to the cabin to pick up Molly.

When they reached the cabin, the boys had jumped out of the SUV and knocked on the door before he could tell them to stay in the car. They were not here for a visit.

"I hope we can have cookies again," Ben said.

"Biscuits," Pete said. "They call cookies *biscuits*."

"Whatever they call them. I hope we can have some more."

"Hey," Jake said. "This isn't a playdate. We're just here to pick up Molly."

"We were just picking up Molly last time too," Pete said. "And we got cookies then."

"Biscuits," Ben said and then laughed.

Jake was shaking his head when the door swung open. And there was Elizabeth, looking as stunning as always.

"Hi, Elizabeth," the boys said before running around her and stepping into the cabin. Immediately the laughter of five children floated through the open windows and door.

"Make yourselves at home," Elizabeth said dryly.

"Sorry about that," Jake said.

"No worries. Come on in."

"I may as well. The boys have already planted themselves in your front room."

"That's fine by me. They're welcome anytime."

He grinned. "Is it me, or are they making more noise now than they did on Saturday?"

"It's the small space. The walls magnify the noise."

"How about we take them outside and let them run around for a while?" he asked. "That is, unless you want us to leave?"

"Of course not. You're welcome to stay."

Ben walked up to them just then, a sweet smile on his face. Jake recognized the look. It was the one he wore whenever he'd been coaxed by Molly and Pete to ask for something.

"Elizabeth, can we have some of the cookies we had last time?"

"Of course. Do you want them now, or would you rather go outside and play first?"

Ben grinned at Elizabeth and held a finger in the air. "I'll be right back." He went back to confer with the others.

Elizabeth and Jake exchanged smiles. Clearly she was not new to the game.

"We want to play first and then have our Tim Tams," Ben declared when he returned. "You do have more, don't you?"

Before Elizabeth could reply, Gianna piped up. "Yes. Our aunt mailed more."

"That's Carly, my sister. She still lives in Australia," Elizabeth explained. "She sends lots of goodies."

"That's nice of her to send you a taste of home," Jake said.

She smirked. "I'm not so sure if it's as innocent as all that. It's her way of reminding me of everything we're missing while we're here."

"I take it that she wants you to move back to Australia."

"We're really close, so yeah, you could say that. We toured together so I know she misses me and the girls."

That was another reminder that Elizabeth's stay could have an expiration date. As if that knowledge was ever far from his mind. That was a big reason he needed to keep his distance. More than that, it was a reason he shouldn't let his kids get attached to her. He didn't want them to be brokenhearted when she went back home.

He frowned. Who was he kidding? The kids weren't worrying about what might happen in the future. The truth was he was trying to protect himself and keep his heart safe.

Jake and Elizabeth followed the kids outside and sat on the wicker rockers as the kids chased each other around the yard. If they were playing tag, they were using rules known only to themselves. They seemed happy, so that was all that mattered.

"I spoke to Rylee today," Elizabeth said.

"About?"

"She wants me to run the Pony Club again. This time for three days. Maybe even a week."

"What are you going to do?"

"I committed for three days. I haven't decided about the other two." She glanced at him. "Would your kids be interested in coming again?"

"Definitely. They had a great time the first time around."

"That's good to hear." Her smile was radiant, and his heart skipped a beat. "Do you think five days would be too much?"

"No. It's summertime. Kids are looking for something to fill the endless hours of free time. Plus, at the Pony Club they get to see their friends again. Add in horses and you have a guaranteed winner."

"How will Molly feel if I run the camp for a week? She loves being my helper. I don't want her to miss out."

"She'll understand. And if it's not an imposition, she

can always help you out at other times during the day. Or even on the weekend."

"It won't be an imposition at all. I know you think she's just playing, but she really is a big help."

Pride swelled in his chest. He knew that his daughter was a treasure, but it was good to know another person recognized it.

They sat in silence for a while, watching the children. After a few minutes, Molly ran over. "We're ready for our cookies now."

"Okay. I have a pitcher of lemonade to go with them," Elizabeth replied, standing.

Jake rose too.

Molly clapped, and Jake noticed her fingernails. They were polished different colors. "Whoa. Let me see your hands."

She grinned and held them out to him. "I forgot to show you. Aren't they cool? Elizabeth did it. Now my nails are just like Gianna's and Lucy's. We all have sunflowers."

"I see."

She preened. "They have spa day. Elizabeth said I can come next time and she'll do all of our nails. Our toenails too. And we'll have fancy drinks with umbrellas and fruit. Doesn't that sound like fun?"

He nodded, trying to keep his feelings from showing on his face. He didn't know how to feel about Elizabeth polishing his daughter's fingernails without his permission. Especially all of these different colors. It might be a small thing to her, but he was Molly's parent. She should have consulted him first. And she certainly should have spoken to him before she invited Molly to this spa day.

"I'll tell everyone to wash their hands so we can have our cookies," Molly said and then ran off.

His daughter hadn't noticed the change in his attitude, but Elizabeth must have. She turned to him, a concerned expression on her face. To her credit, she did seem remorseful. "I don't know what I've done, but I've done something to get on your bad side. Is it the manicure or the fact that I invited Molly to spa day with me and my girls? Why are you angry with me?"

Chapter Seven

Elizabeth watched as Jake pondered her question. It hadn't been a particularly difficult one in her mind, so he must've been struggling to find just the right words so as not to offend her. "Jake, just say what you're feeling. I won't break. I'm stronger than I look."

"I guess it might be a combination."

"I'll simply remove the polish. No problem," she said. "Rescinding the invitation to spa day will be harder, but I'll handle it."

"And turn me into the bad guy?"

"Not at all. I'll explain to Molly that I should have asked you before I polished her nails."

"That would have been nice."

She sighed at the restrained anger in his voice. "It never occurred to me that it would be a problem. I've been giving my daughters mani-pedis for a while. It started as a way to trim their nails with the least amount of hassle. Over time it became one of their favorite things for us to do together. Mine too. Molly is the first person they invited to join us."

He blew out a breath. "Do you think I'm overreacting?"

"Does it matter what I think? You're her father, and what you say goes."

Jake shoved his hands into his pockets. "Don't take off the polish. She really seems to like the way her nails look."

"Of course she does. Most girls like having fancy nails. It makes them feel pretty and a little bit grown up."

"I'm being a jerk, and it has nothing to do with you," he said.

"Then why do I feel like it does?"

"One of the mothers at karate is using our boys to try to get close to me." His cheeks grew ruddy as he spoke. Clearly the entire situation embarrassed him.

"And you thought that I was doing the same with Molly? Are you *kidding me*?" Her voice rose on the last words. She looked over her shoulder. Luckily the kids were still crowded into the bathroom washing their hands. Even so, she lowered her voice. "Are you out of your mind?"

His expression was sheepish. "It sounds ridiculous when you say it out loud."

"That's because it is ridiculous. I'm not interested in a relationship with you, Jake."

Her words sounded harsh in her own ears, and she knew she could have been more diplomatic, but she didn't retract them. She didn't want there to be any confusion. Apparently he thought she wanted more than friendship with him and that she was sneaky enough to use his daughter in her plan. That he actually thought she could be so devious hurt her soul.

He winced. "I got it."

"Do you?" she asked. "Because my life is in flux. I don't need another complication. And that's what a relationship with you would be. I'm trying to decide whether to go back to Australia or start over here in America. That's change enough for me." She sighed. She might as well lay her cards on the table. "I like you as a friend. But if I'm being totally honest, I might even find you a little bit attractive."

"Just a little bit?" he asked with a wicked grin that made her heart skip a beat.

She ignored the sensation as well as his comment. "But my situation remains the same. I might not even be in this country in a couple of months."

"As long as we're being honest, I find you more than a little bit attractive."

His words made her knees tremble, and she hoped he didn't notice the extra effort it took for her to remain standing. "Well, then."

What was she supposed to do with that bit of knowledge? The only thing she could do. Shove it aside and forget about it. She could only hope he would do the same.

"That's not the only reason I acted like a jerk. And it probably isn't the main one."

Elizabeth blew out a breath. "Then what is?"

"Because it's hard to see my little girl growing up. Watching her grow away from me. There are times when I don't understand her. Times when I can't give her what she needs. If her mother was here, she would know what to say and do."

Elizabeth nodded.

"I'm so proud of the young lady she is becoming. But seeing her new manicure only emphasized that I don't have the foggiest notion about what is important to her. I would never have thought about a mani/pedi as being something that mattered to her. And you've only known her for a little while, and you knew what she would like."

"I understand. It's hard to watch them grow up."

"I wish Maggie was here. Not just to help with the hard situations, but to see just how wonderful her kids have become. And she's not." Jake's voice broke on the last words, and Elizabeth's heart ached for him. She could relate to that grief.

"I feel the same way about Arlo. But holding on to the pain and anger isn't good for any of us."

"I know. That's why I'm trying to look to the future." He moved closer and her heart began to thud. Their eyes met and the emotion she saw in his made it impossible for her to look away. The surroundings seemed to fade, making it feel as if they were the only two people in the world.

"Are we having our snack or not?" Pete said, running over to them and bringing an end to their true confession session. "We washed our hands."

"Coming right up," Elizabeth said, not sure if she was relieved or upset by the interruption. "Let's go, kids."

The group hustled into the kitchen and gathered around the table.

"Does everyone want the same cookies as last time?"

"Yes," they all said loudly.

Jake poured the lemonade, then stood aside as Elizabeth opened packages of Tim Tams. What she wouldn't give to eat a handful of the chocolate deliciousness now.

"Do you remember what everyone wanted?" he asked.

"Of course."

She felt his eyes on her as she passed out the treats. Once the kids had been served, she handed Jake several mint cookies.

"I'm impressed," he said.

"You should be." She looked around. As before, the kids had left a chair for her and Jake to share. The idea of sitting that close to him made her shiver. It had felt so good to sit beside him, his leg pressed against hers. Just recalling how good it had been to feel the heat from his body wrap around her made her shiver. Given the fact that she'd just confessed to being attracted to him, it would be best not to risk that kind of intimate contact again. "Come on—let's have our snack in the main room."

Jake nodded and followed her. Luckily he didn't try to make conversation as they ate. Instead they spent time alone with their thoughts. There was plenty for them to contemplate. Elizabeth was still reeling from admitting that she was attracted to Jake. She couldn't believe she'd just gone and volunteered that information. Not that it mattered. She had been honest when she'd told him she had too much going on in her life to consider a relationship.

Even so, she was thrilled to know that he was attracted to her. Not that anything could come from that. There were so many differences between them. A big one was their way of raising their children. She would never allow her daughters to keep their bedrooms as messy as he let Ben and Pete keep theirs. Gianna and Lucy made their beds each morning before they got dressed. They knew to toss their dirty clothes into the hamper and to put away their clean clothes. While neatness mattered to her, it clearly wasn't a big deal to Jake. It was good that the differences were appearing now before she and Jake got in too deep.

When the kids finished their snacks, Gianna and Lucy placed their dishes in the sink.

Molly did the same, then instructed her brothers to follow.

"Say thank-you," Jake said.

"Thank you," his kids chorused.

"You're quite welcome," Elizabeth replied.

"And on that note, we need to get going." Jake corralled his kids, led them out the door, and into his SUV.

Once the vehicle was out of sight, the girls turned to Elizabeth. "Can we watch the telly?"

"Sure."

When they were settled in front of the television Elizabeth grabbed her phone. Her mind was a mess, and she needed to talk. If she was back home in Australia, she would call Carly. But given the time difference, she couldn't. Luckily she had other sisters close by that she could talk to.

Taking one last look at her girls who were absorbed in their program, Elizabeth headed to the relative privacy of the kitchen. She was close enough to keep an eye on the girls but far enough away not to be overheard. Before she could punch in any of her sisters' numbers, her phone rang. When the name popped on the screen she smiled and answered.

"You must have ESP," she said to her sister Faith.

"Why do you say that?"

"I was about to give you a ring. Well, you, Amy, and Tori."

"Oh. Sister conference call. That must mean that the topic is serious. Should I add them in?"

Elizabeth hesitated. Faith had probably just called to catch up with her. If it was only the two of them on the line, they could do just that. If they added in Tori and Amy, she would end up discussing her feelings. But wasn't that what she wanted to do? Needed to do?

Besides, did she want to hide from her sisters? She'd been trying to hide from herself, and judging from her dreams about Jake, that wasn't working so well.

"Go ahead and add them. I could use all the help I can get."

"That sounds ominous," Faith said. "Hold on."

In less than a minute, Tori and Amy were on the line.

"What's up?" Tori asked.

"I just need a dose of sister common sense."

"Oh, it must be a man," Amy said.

Tori and Faith laughed.

"So who is it?" Amy asked.

"Talk about taking the bull by the horn."

"Why waste time?" she said. "You're going to tell us eventually. Besides, the girls will be demanding your attention soon, so there's no time to waste."

"I don't even know where to start," Elizabeth said. "I'm confused. And truthfully, I may be getting ahead of myself."

"So what? We're your sisters. It's not as if this conversation is going to go any further than us," Faith said.

"I know that." Elizabeth sucked in a breath and then blew it out. "I met a man."

Her sisters began to talk all at once, but she managed to hear Tori say, "About time."

"What's his name?" Amy asked.

"Where did you meet him?" This from Tori.

"Let her talk," Faith said.

"His name is Jake McCreery. I met him at the Pony Club." When nobody said anything, Elizabeth continued, "He's a widower with three kids."

"Wow. Three kids. Plus your two. Talk about a full house," Amy said.

"Nobody is talking about joining families," Elizabeth said, nipping that kind of talk in the bud. "We haven't even gone on a date yet. Nor has he asked me to."

"How long ago did his wife die?" Faith asked quietly, taking the conversation in another direction.

"Six years. She died giving birth to their youngest son, Ben."

"How sad," Tori said.

"That had to be hard on him," Amy said.

"I imagine it was," Elizabeth replied. From her experience she knew *hard* didn't begin to describe it.

"Has he been single since then? Maybe he isn't over his wife. If that's the case, you could be walking into a bunch of pain," Faith added.

"I don't know whether he is or not. Since I can't say I'm all the way over Arlo, I understand if he isn't. I know Arlo is gone and won't be coming back..." Before her sisters could comment she continued, "I'll always love him. He owns a piece of my heart that will never belong to another man. So I understand if a part of Jake will always love Maggie."

"So what's the problem?" Tori asked.

"Why does there have to be a problem?" Elizabeth countered as if she hadn't wanted to talk things out with her sisters.

"Because there's always a problem with love and romance," Faith said.

"It wouldn't be worth it if it came too easily," Tori said.

"There is no love or romance. I'm not in love with Jake."

"But you like him," Amy said.

"Is that silly? I don't even know him, but I dreamed about him."

"Aw." Tori sighed.

"I feel as if I'm losing Arlo. His memory is fading. This morning I couldn't remember the sound of his voice."

"It's been two years," Amy said softly. "You're entitled to move on. In fact, it's not healthy for you to keep living in the past."

"I'm not living in the past. But I don't want to pretend that my husband didn't exist. I can't act as if our love didn't sustain me."

"Nobody is saying that you should forget Arlo," Faith said.

"Arlo loved you," Tori said. "He knew you loved him.

But he would want you to find love again. He would want you to be happy."

"I am happy. My girls make me happy."

"What about Jake? Does he make you happy?" Tori asked.

Did he? They had a good time together the other day. She'd enjoyed talking to him today despite hitting a speed bump.

"He's easy to be with," Elizabeth settled for saying.

"That's not exactly an answer."

"He has his own issues. Women started pursuing him a couple of months after his wife died. Circling him like vultures."

"Talk about tacky," Faith said.

"And disgusting," Amy added.

"Yes. I offered to include his daughter in spa day. He thought I was using Molly in order to get close to him."

"Did he accuse you of that?" Amy asked, sounding offended on Elizabeth's behalf.

"Not in so many words. We talked about it, and he admitted that he'd jumped to the wrong conclusion."

"If you decide to have a relationship, no doubt you'll have more misunderstandings. I can't imagine it will be easy since you've both lost a beloved spouse. Plus you each have children to raise," Tori said.

Elizabeth sighed. "That about sums it up."

"I don't know what you're thinking," Amy said, "but I for one think that you should give the relationship a try."

"Even with all the possible landmines?" Elizabeth asked.

"Yes." Amy's reply came without hesitation.

"Why?"

"Lots of reasons," Amy said.

"Give me one."

"You deserve to be happy. So do the girls," she said.

"And Jake is the first man you've been attracted to since Arlo died," Tori added.

"And most importantly, a romance will keep you in Montana," Faith said. "If things work out with Jake, you'll settle down here and the four of us will be together again. Who knows, Carly might even decide that she wants to move back to the States."

"That might be wishful thinking on your part," Elizabeth said. "Carly absolutely loves living in Australia."

"I notice that you didn't reply to any of the other things we said," Amy said.

"It's just so hard. I loved Arlo so much. I don't want to put him in the past. Getting together with Jake requires me to do that."

"Weren't you just saying something different?" Amy asked.

"I was. I know. Everything is so confusing. Whenever I think about Jake, I feel guilty. A relationship with him feels like the ultimate betrayal of Arlo."

"It isn't," Faith said.

"If you had been the one to die, would you want Arlo to mourn you for the rest of his life?" Tori asked.

"You better believe it," Elizabeth said, giving a watery chuckle. Her eyes were brimming with unshed tears, and she needed to lighten the moment. She didn't want to break down. She'd cried a river these past two years.

"You know we don't believe that," Tori said.

"I know," Elizabeth said. "It just feels different somehow."

"You can't ignore your feelings and hope they go away. You have to go through them," Amy said.

"We had such a good life. I can't believe that it's over. And my girls… Gianna and Lucy had the best father two girls could ever want." She gulped. "I just can't believe that they only got to have three years with him. They barely remember him."

"But you'll keep him alive for them," Faith said.

"But if I get involved with another man…"

"That won't change anything." Tori sighed. "I wish I was there so I could give you a big hug."

"Me too," Amy said.

"Well, what's stopping us?" Faith asked.

"Nothing," Amy said. "We're coming over."

"That's not necessary," Elizabeth said. "I'm fine."

"I'm sure you are. But it would be good to have a little time together. I'll stop and get us some takeout," Faith said. "I know that Gianna and Lucy would love to see us."

"If you insist," Elizabeth said.

"We do."

"Then come on over."

She hung up the phone and smiled. It was good to be here with her sisters. But would that closeness be enough to make her leave Australia and the only home the girls had ever known?

"So, are you going to get this one or not?"

Jake looked into the face of his ranch foreman. There was a confused look on Gerard's face.

"What one?"

"The steer."

Jake blinked then ordered himself to get back in the game. He glanced at the steer currently heading for a ditch a few feet away. "Yeah. I got it."

He spurred Lancelot into action, chasing down the stray steer and guiding it back to the rest of the herd.

They were moving the cattle from one grazing area to

another. The cows were huge, and even riding a well-trained horse who knew when and how to move, Jake could get hurt if he didn't pay attention. And he was definitely distracted now. He had been all day.

The moment his alarm clock had gone off, he'd started to think about Elizabeth. As he'd fried bacon and eggs for the kids before his parents had picked them up to spend the day in town, he'd recalled how beautiful she'd looked the last time he'd seen her. He'd completely lost track of what he'd been doing as he'd fantasized about spending time with her.

And he was doing it again.

"You look like you have something on your mind," Gerard said as Jake rejoined him.

Gerard and Jake had been good friends since they were kids. Gerard had supported Jake in the miserable days following Maggie's death, listening as Jake raged against fate. He knew that anything he told Gerard would remain between the two of them. But he also knew that talking about Elizabeth now would only distract him even more.

"Maybe."

"And you don't want to talk about it."

Jake nodded. "I need to stay focused on this drive."

"Good enough." Gerard nodded and rode away.

Normally Jake loved cattle drives. There was something so peaceful about being on horseback and crossing the acres of his ranch. Today, with the bright shining sun in the clear blue sky, should have been next to heaven. But instead of enjoying it, he couldn't keep his head in the game. All he could think about was Elizabeth.

Finally they got the herd to the pasture. Gerard rode over to Jake. "We can take it from here. Your parents will be bringing the kids back in a couple of hours."

"Thanks." Jake turned Lancelot and they rode across the

ranch until he reached the house and rustled up something for his dinner. His parents would feed the kids so that was one less thing Jake needed to worry about.

He was polishing off his steak sandwich when his mother called, telling him that the kids wanted to sleep over. "We'll bring them home first thing in the morning."

"Thanks, Mom."

"Enjoy your quiet time," she said before ending the call.

Jake leaned back in his chair and closed his eyes. He hadn't been this preoccupied since he and Maggie had first gotten together. She had been the only woman who could make his heart sing. Over time he'd learned to live without music in his life, learning to endure the silence.

Now Elizabeth was changing all of that. His body hummed whenever she was around. She was the first person that he thought of when he awoke, the last person that he thought of at night. Even now he was sitting here thinking about her when there were several other things he could be doing. Why was she relentlessly on his mind? She was only his friend. Friendship was fine with him. Did he want her to play a bigger role in his life? Maybe. But only if there was a place for him in her life.

He sighed. It was time to be honest with himself. Lying was a surefire way to make a mistake—something his children couldn't afford for him to do. Pretending he wasn't attracted to Elizabeth was a way of lying to himself. Admitting his feelings had lifted a weight from his shoulders. His ego had been boosted to hear that she was attracted to him. Even an old bachelor dad like him wanted to appeal to women. Well, not *women* exactly. Woman. Elizabeth Hawkins.

He liked their easy way of communicating. As a widow, she was uniquely qualified to understand his complex and confusing emotions. She could relate to wanting to get close but being afraid to move.

Guilt roiled his stomach. He shouldn't have been thinking that way about Elizabeth. It was as if he was putting her on the same level as Maggie. That was wrong. Maggie belonged in her own category. How could he feel as connected to a woman he barely knew as he had with his beloved wife?

Jake rubbed a hand over his face. Talking to himself was getting him nowhere. He was only going in circles. He'd gotten accustomed to the loneliness that came with being a single parent, but he still missed having someone to bounce ideas off. Someone who could suggest a solution he hadn't considered. That was what Maggie had always done for him. What they'd always done for each other.

But Maggie was gone. And he needed to talk to someone he trusted about his attraction to Elizabeth and the confusing emotions she awoke in him. He checked the time. No doubt, Gerard had just gotten home and was spending precious time with his own family. Jake didn't want to disturb him. But it was still early enough for him to call his sister, so he punched in her number.

Bethany answered on the second ring. "What's up?"

"I just felt like talking to an adult. Is now a good time?"

"Of course. I just finished learning a new song." Bethany was a wedding singer extraordinaire and in great demand. Jake hadn't been exaggerating when he'd told Elizabeth that his sister had enough talent for two people.

Bethany and Jake had always been close. They'd grown even closer after Maggie's death. Back then, he'd depended on her—perhaps more than he should have. When he'd been shrouded by grief, she had been a comfort and a shoulder to lean on. She'd stepped in and cared for the kids when he'd been paralyzed by sorrow. If not for Bethany, he wouldn't have made it through those rough early months.

But he'd never faced a situation like this one.

Now that Jake had someone willing to listen, he didn't know how or where to start.

"It must be serious if you can't find the words." Bethany's voice was a mixture of amusement and concern.

"You could say that."

"It can only be one thing. You met a woman."

He knew that his sister was astute, so he shouldn't have been surprised that she'd put her finger on his problem right away. But he was. "I won't bother to ask how you guessed that."

Bethany's whoop was a sound of complete joy. "It's about time."

"What makes you say that?"

"It's been six years since you lost Maggie. I know that you loved her with your whole heart, but nobody expects you to be alone forever. It's okay for you to move on. That's what she would have wanted for you."

"You've told me that before."

"I know. But this is the first time that you seem to be taking my words to heart," Bethany said. "So who is this woman?"

"Her name is Elizabeth. Elizabeth Hawkins."

"Is she related to the Hawkins rodeo family?"

"Yes. She competes in the rodeo too but in Australia."

"Wow. She's a long way from home."

"I know." He explained how she'd come to Montana.

"Is she staying in Bronco?" Bethany asked.

"That's the question. I wish I knew the answer to it."

"Have you asked her?"

"We talked about it briefly. She doesn't know what she

plans to do in the future. She's taking it day by day." Jake sighed. "Elizabeth is a widow with twin five-year-old daughters."

"Oh. When did her husband die?"

"Two years ago. She's trying to figure out her next move."

"Something that you know all about," she said.

"All too well."

"And if she decides to stay? Then what?"

"I don't know." Jake looked up at the ceiling as if the answer would somehow magically appear there. It didn't. "I know that Maggie is gone, but it feels wrong to even think about sharing the rest of my life with someone else. Helping to raise another woman's children and letting her help me to raise Molly, Pete, and Ben in Maggie's place."

"She wouldn't be taking Maggie's place any more than you would be taking her husband's. You'll each have to make your own places in the kids' lives if you decide to make a go of it."

"Should I even try?" he asked.

"That's not a question I can answer. Nor should I."

"Point taken."

"But I will say that you're lucky to have found someone worthy of taking a chance with."

"I'm sorry that things didn't work out for you and Rexx." Rexx had been the bass player in Bethany's band and definitely not worthy of her.

"That whole relationship was a mistake from the beginning."

There was something about the tone of her voice that gave Jake pause. She didn't sound like herself. He immediately sprang into big-brother mode. "What's wrong?"

"Nothing."

"Don't tell me nothing. I can tell that something's wrong,"

he said. "You've listened to my troubles for six years. If I needed anything, all I had to do was call. Surely you can let me do the same for you."

Bethany sighed. "I'm good, Jake. Really."

Jake knew that she was holding something back, but he couldn't force her to tell him. Nor would he try to. He respected her too much for that. She was entitled to have her own secrets. "Okay."

"What do the kids think of Elizabeth?"

"They like her. They've talked about her nonstop since they met. She hired Molly as her mother's helper."

"Considering the way Molly tends to mother Pete and Ben, that's right up her alley," Bethany said. "How does she like it?"

"She loves it. Molly is so proud to earn her own money. And she really likes being around Elizabeth's daughters."

"I'm sure. Pete and Ben are good kids, but Molly needs other little girls to play with. Living on the ranch can make getting together with her friends that much more difficult."

"I'm a rancher," Jake said somewhat defensively. "I can't move to town and still make a living."

"I'm not accusing you of doing anything wrong And I certainly don't expect you to sell the ranch. I'm sure Molly doesn't either. But the fact remains that she is the only female in the house. Being around Elizabeth and her daughters must be nice for her. That's all I meant. And I think you know that."

"I do."

He was quiet for a while.

"What aren't you telling me? What's bugging you?" Bethany asked.

"She polished Molly's nails and styled her hair to match Gianna's and Lucy's."

"That's a good thing."

"I know," he said. "It just made me feel… I don't know how to explain it."

"It made you feel like you're failing in some ways because you're a man."

"Yes. It never occurred to me that she might want a manicure. And I'm not talking about a plain manicure. Her nails are all different colors. Elizabeth painted sunflowers on a couple of them."

"I bet Molly was over the moon."

"She was."

"Most dads don't think of things like that, so don't beat yourself up over it. Heck, it never occurred to me, and I'm a woman."

"Thank you for saying that. It makes me feel a little bit better."

"Good. And you should know there will be times in the future when you're not going to think of things. Not just for Molly, but for the boys too. You can't know everything that matters to them."

"Maggie would have."

"No, she wouldn't. Maggie was a woman. Flesh and blood just like you and complete with flaws. You have built her up in your mind to mythical proportions, but she didn't have magical powers. She didn't see or know all."

"So, you're telling me what?"

"Two things. First, go easy on yourself. You're a good dad."

He smiled. "What's the second thing?"

"Remember Maggie the way she was. Otherwise no woman will ever be able to compare. Give Elizabeth a real chance."

Jake nodded even though his sister couldn't see him. He'd asked for her advice. Now he needed to follow it. "I will."

Chapter Eight

"This is going to be so much fun," Ben said as he raced across the sidewalk to the doors of the convention center.

"Wait until we catch up," Jake called even though Molly and Pete were hot on Ben's heels. The kids were so excited to attend the Pony Club again. They'd been awake for hours and had asked him repeatedly when they would be leaving. Judging by how fast they were running, they couldn't wait another second.

Jake jogged the last few steps in order to catch up with the kids. It was unlikely they would be in any danger, but he didn't want his kids to run amok. And while he didn't worry about other people's opinions about most things, he didn't want to look like a bad father. Especially in front of Elizabeth, whose girls had to be the best mannered kids he'd ever met.

He laughed to himself at that ridiculous notion. He wasn't auditioning for the role of Lucy's and Gianna's stepfather. He had his hands full with just three kids. It took supreme effort to give each of them individual time and attention. He couldn't see how it would be possible to divide his time five ways. Given his failure to recognize Molly's changing interests, the last thing he should have been considering was taking on more girls.

"We know where to go," Pete said.

"I know. But let's stay together."

Pete huffed out a breath, but he stayed with the group. When they reached the arena, the kids spotted their friends. Before Jake could stop them, Pete and Ben dashed away to join them. He saw a couple of girls who were in Molly's class.

"Hey, isn't that Emma over there?" he tried, but he couldn't remember the name of the other little girl.

"Yeah. And Jessie." Molly waved and continued to look around. Then she smiled. "I see Elizabeth and Lucy and Gianna. I'm going over there."

She stepped away, and he followed. Molly stopped and stared at him. "I don't need you to go with me. I'm not a baby."

"I know that. I just wanted to say hello to Elizabeth. After all, she's my friend too."

Molly narrowed her eyes for a moment as she considered his words. He didn't know if she was focused on the fact that he called Elizabeth his friend or whether she thought he was using Elizabeth's presence as an excuse to follow her. She nodded. "Okay."

Elizabeth's back was to him, and he took a moment to study her. She was wearing a rodeo shirt covered with sponsor patches and jeans that her round backside filled out nicely. The fringed pink shirt was tied at the waist, emphasizing its small size. Her pink cowboy boots had fringe around the top, adding style and fashion. She might've been dressed to ride a horse, but Jake just thought she looked hot.

She turned just then, and their eyes met. He was close enough to notice her chest rise with her quick intake of breath before she smiled. Her eyes sparkled with pleasure, and his heart leaped in response. When Molly reached Elizabeth, she ran straight into her arms. As they hugged, Jake smiled. Elizabeth said something that didn't reach his ears, but whatever it was made Molly laugh.

When Jake reached the floor, he walked over to Elizabeth, wishing that he could give her a hug too. Of course, that was out of the question. They didn't have that type of relationship. Even so, his arms ached to hold her.

"How are you?" Elizabeth asked. She stepped closer, and her sweet scent teased his senses.

"How do I look?" he countered, suddenly feeling playful.

She paused and gave him a once-over, starting with his booted feet and letting her gaze travel over him until it reached his black cowboy hat. "Honestly? You look like you've been wrestling with three kids who were eager to get to the Pony Club."

The laugh that burst from his lips was loud and quite unexpected. A couple of parents turned to look at him. "That bad, huh? I hope nobody else noticed."

"Only someone who has been dealing with excited twin girls for hours would notice, so you're safe."

He shook his head. "You look too good for me to believe that."

She laughed. "It's the lighting in here. And makeup."

Her words gave him the excuse he needed to study her face. She didn't appear to have an ounce of makeup on her glowing brown skin. She removed her cowboy hat, brushed her wavy hair over her shoulder, and then replaced the hat.

An attractive woman walked over to them. "Sorry to interrupt, but I just wanted to let you know we're ready whenever you are."

"Thanks," Elizabeth said. She looked at Jake. "This is my sister Faith. Faith, this is Jake, my new friend. His daughter, Molly, is my mother's helper."

Faith smiled and held out a hand. "It's nice to meet you, Jake."

"Likewise." He shook her hand and then looked back at Elizabeth. "I'll get out of your way so you can get started."

"I'll talk to you later," she promised.

Something to look forward to.

Jake nodded and walked away. He spotted Pete and Ben with a group of kids, and he took a seat in the middle of the arena where he could keep an eye on them. Elizabeth walked up to a microphone and asked for quiet. In an instant, you could hear a pin drop.

She welcomed the campers, then called the kids by name to form groups. The session would last for three hours each day. Several parents had left, and Jake knew that he could run out to Bronco Feed and Ranch Supply. He didn't often have time to himself, and there were many errands he could run while the kids were otherwise occupied. Instead of taking advantage of the free time, he stayed seated. Elizabeth was enchanting, and he enjoyed looking at her.

She was quite gifted, and the kids were hanging on her every word. She helped each of them with the horses, kneeling down in front of one little girl of about seven who appeared to be afraid. The girl backed away, and Elizabeth stood. Before the child could bolt, Gianna walked over and took her hand. Then Lucy went over to the horse. Either the twins were quite persuasive or the little girl's ego would not allow her to fear something that two younger kids didn't. Regardless, after a moment, she reached out and touched the horse.

Although he had absolutely no reason to be proud—he had nothing to do with the twins or how they were raised— he was filled with pride. Jake glanced at Molly, who also watched the scene. She seemed a bit lost, as if unsure of her role. He'd explained to her that she would be a camper and not Elizabeth's helper, but he wasn't sure she'd understood what that difference entailed.

Elizabeth walked over to Molly and put a hand on her shoulder. She said something, and Molly nodded and smiled. Then Molly began talking to another girl, helping her to become comfortable with the horses. Obviously Elizabeth had understood Molly's feelings and known how to make her feel needed. His daughter blossomed with Elizabeth's attention.

Maybe he needed to reconsider his stance about adding a woman to his family.

"I like being your assistant like Lucy and Gianna," Molly said, smiling up at Elizabeth.

"I like having you as my assistant. You're doing such a good job," Elizabeth said.

"I tried to do my hair the way you combed it the other day, but I couldn't. And the little braids came out. So I had to do it the old way."

"If it's okay with your father I can comb your hair after camp today."

"Why wouldn't it be okay with Daddy? He never says anything about my hair."

Elizabeth didn't want to mention the discussion that she and Jake had had the other day about Molly's nails, so she hedged. "I know. But he may be busy with the ranch after club ends. We want to be considerate."

"I get it now. I suppose we have to talk to Daddy about it," Molly said. "Can you do it? He won't say no if you ask."

Elizabeth wasn't so sure about that, but when she glanced down at Molly's hopeful face, she couldn't do anything but agree. "Sure."

"And when is spa day? Some of my nails are starting to chip. I saw Emma and Jessie in town the other day, and I showed them my nails. They liked them so much. They wanted to know if you could do their nails too, but I told them no. It was only for me and Lucy and Gianna. I told them they needed to ask their own moms."

Their own moms. Was Molly starting to view Elizabeth as a surrogate mother? Or had Elizabeth read too much into that comment? After all, given that Emma and Jessie had mothers, that was a true statement. "We'll talk to your father about doing your hair and nails. Maybe we can show him the designs before we do them. Just to get his opinion."

Molly's nose wrinkled, but she didn't say anything.

Elizabeth patted her shoulder. "Well, let's get back to work. There are lots of campers depending on us to show them what to do."

In addition to teaching the kids about horses and giving them short rides around the arena, Elizabeth talked about her life on the rodeo. There were lots of questions, and she happily answered all of them. By the time the day ended, she was talked out. The campers moaned and groaned when she announced that parents had arrived, but she reminded them that they would be meeting again in two days.

Although Jake was sitting on the bleachers as he had throughout the session, Molly didn't go over to him. Instead she hung by Elizabeth's side, playing with Gianna and Lucy. Once everyone was gone—including Faith, Tori, and Amy, who'd waved and indicated they would call her later—Elizabeth led the girls over to where Jake sat with his sons.

He stood up as they drew near. Gianna and Lucy ran over, and Gianna grabbed one of Jake's legs. "Can you carry me on your shoulders again? And Lucy too?"

"Wait a minute," Elizabeth said. "Did you even say hi before you asked for a favor?"

"Oops. Hi, Jake. Do you want to carry me on your shoulders?"

Jake gave Gianna a lopsided grin that made Elizabeth's stomach tumble. "Of course I would like to give each of you a ride. Who wouldn't?"

Gianna shrugged.

"Elizabeth wants to ask you something," Molly said.

"Is that right? Well, I'm all ears."

Pete burst into laughter. "That would be funny. You wouldn't have any hands or legs if you were all ears."

Ben gave his brother a quizzical look before walking over to Elizabeth and grabbing her hand. He gave her a snaggletoothed smile. This sweet little boy was finding his way into her heart. "Hi, Elizabeth. Club was fun. We should do it every day."

"Ben," Molly said sharply, "Elizabeth was trying to talk to Daddy."

"Sorry," he said, his smile just as wide as before. Clearly nothing bothered him.

"Is it something you want me to ask in private?" Elizabeth asked Molly. "Or can everyone hear?"

"It's not a secret," Molly said. "I don't care who hears."

"In that case… Jake, would it be okay if I combed Molly's hair in a different style? I have a couple of ideas that she might like."

His brow wrinkled in confusion as if unsure why she was asking him this question. Then his face cleared as he must have recalled their previous conversation. "Of course. That would be fine."

"And Elizabeth wants to show you how she wants to do my nails on spa day. I told her you don't know anything about fingernail polish, but she still wants you to see the design. To be considerate."

Regret was visible on Jake's face, and Elizabeth realized that he had actually meant it when he'd apologized. He hadn't simply been trying to get past an unpleasant moment. That raised him a few notches in her book.

"Molly is right," he said. "I don't know much about nails. Do whatever you think would be best."

Elizabeth smiled. "I have so many ideas for our next spa day."

"Why don't we get to come to your house like Molly does?" Ben asked.

"I'm working," Molly pointed out. "Besides, you're a boy. We're doing girl stuff."

"Can you guys come over to our house?" he asked. "That way we can do regular kid stuff."

"Yeah. I want to play in the tree house and on the swings," Gianna said.

"Me too," Lucy chimed in.

"You can come over today, right, Dad?" Pete said. "We aren't doing anything fun."

"Maybe Elizabeth and the girls have plans."

"No, we don't," Lucy said. "We can come over today, right, Mummy?"

Elizabeth glanced hopelessly at Jake, then looked at her daughters. "It's not polite to invite yourself to someone else's house."

"I didn't," Gianna said. "Pete invited us."

"So he did. In that case, if it's okay with Jake, it's okay with me."

"Say yes, Daddy," Molly said, and the other kids added their pleas.

"Sure. I can throw something on the grill again."

"I feel as if I should add something. Fruit salad or some kind of dessert."

Jake shook his head. "That's not necessary. Your company will be enough."

"Are you sure?" Elizabeth asked.

"Positive. If it makes you feel better, you can cook next time."

For five kids? "Or I'll get takeaway."

Once the kids decided they wanted a "girl car" and a "boy car," they ran outside to the vehicles and piled in. Elizabeth had a vague idea of how to get to his ranch, but she felt more comfortable following his lead.

The girls whispered to each other on the ride, talking too quietly for Elizabeth to catch more than a word or two every now and again. Not that she tried. How much mischief could three little girls dream up, especially when two of them were only five?

Elizabeth let her mind wander as she drove. Naturally it found its way to Jake. He was beginning to occupy her thoughts more frequently, popping into her mind seemingly at will and at the most inopportune times. One minute she would be concentrating on the task at hand and the next she would find herself smiling, thinking of something he'd said. Or the way he moved. He didn't so much walk as he sauntered. She couldn't count the number of times she remembered admiring the perfect way his shirt fit his muscular chest and shoulders. She'd spent way too much time imagining how good it would feel to be wrapped in his strong arms. How heavenly it would feel to be kissed by him.

Elizabeth felt her temperature rise, and she fanned herself with her free hand. She shouldn't be thinking this way about Jake, especially while driving. Truth be told, she shouldn't be fantasizing about making out with him at any time. She had two daughters to raise and major decisions to make. The last thing she needed was to add a further complication to the mix. She should be trying to clarify her thinking, not muddying up the water.

Even with the self-discipline she'd developed from her years on the rodeo circuit she didn't have the power to keep from daydreaming about Jake. As her sisters had so aptly pointed out, she was a living and breathing, flesh and blood woman. The desires and needs that had been dormant for the past two years were awake and demanding attention. She was relieved to no longer be numb, but she would prefer her feelings come on gradually and not hot and heavy as they were doing. But you couldn't always get what you wanted.

Jake signaled and turned into his driveway, so she did the same. They parked, and the kids scrambled from the cars. Talking as if they hadn't seen each other in ages, they ran to the porch. Then they turned away from the front door.

"We're going to play on the swings," Molly announced. As one, the kids raced back down the stairs and around the house to the backyard. Their happy laughter floated to the front of the house.

"I like that sound," Elizabeth said to Jake.

"So do I." He unlocked the front door, and they went inside and headed straight for the kitchen.

"My girls have changed a lot since they've gotten to know your children."

"I hope the change is positive."

"It is. I think they're becoming who they would have been if they hadn't lost Arlo. They're more carefree. Lucy isn't as quiet as she'd become. I love to see it."

"Maybe that's a sign that you should move to the States."

"I don't believe in signs," Elizabeth said.

"What do you believe in?" he asked.

"Oh. That's a good question." She paused. "I believe in facts. I believe that hard work pays off."

"I can agree with that." He opened the freezer and pulled out a box of frozen burgers and a couple packages of hot dogs.

"I hope we haven't put you in a bad position."

"You haven't," Jake said.

"If you have the ingredients, I could make potato salad. That is, if your kids eat it."

"They aren't picky. I haven't had potato salad in longer than I can recall, so I would love some."

They gathered the ingredients, then Elizabeth set the potatoes in a pot of water to boil. While the potatoes cooked, she chopped an onion. At the same time, Jake prepped the meat for the grill. The kitchen was spacious, yet on more than one occasion she found herself close enough to Jake to touch. Although she managed to resist the temptation, she wasn't above breathing in his scent whenever he was near. He smelled so good. Like clean male and fresh air. It was enough to weaken her knees.

"Let's sit outside while the potatoes boil," Jake said.

"That sounds good to me," Elizabeth said, following him to the patio and then taking a seat at the table. She leaned back and then glanced over to where the kids were playing. It was a relief to know there was another adult looking out for her daughters. Jake could be thinking the same thing right now about his kids. Two adults were definitely better than one.

"We work well together," Jake said, saying what she'd just thought.

"We do."

"I think we might play together well too."

She glanced over at him. He was looking at her, a gleam in his eyes and a smile tugging on his lips. She leaned onto her hand. "Do tell."

His eyes widened as he realized how suggestive his words might have sounded. "That didn't come out quite right."

"Then say what you meant."

"I think it would be fun to go on a date. Just the two of us. We can go to dinner. Or a movie. Or both. You could bring Gianna and Lucy over here, and I could get my sister to babysit."

"That sounds nice," Elizabeth said. "But I can get one of my sisters to keep Gianna and Lucy. We wouldn't want to overwhelm Bethany with five kids. Besides, my sisters are always telling me that they want to spend more time with my girls. I think this is part of their plan to convince me to stay in Montana."

"In that case, definitely call one of them."

"I guess I don't have to ask where you stand on my dilemma."

"Is it a dilemma?" Jake asked. He sobered, setting all joking aside for the moment.

"Maybe *dilemma* isn't the right word. But it is a big decision. I don't want to make the wrong one."

"Instead of thinking in terms of right and wrong, why not think of it a different way?"

"If you know another way, please let me know."

"How about looking at it as a now and later decision?" he said. "Look at it as a question of what you do now. Remember, it's not an unchangeable decision. If you decide to stay and it doesn't turn out the way you want, you can always go back. And vice versa."

She shook her head. Why hadn't it occurred to her to look

at it this way? All her life she'd been accused of making mountains out of molehills. Making problems bigger than they actually were. Yes, deciding whether to move to the States or go back home to Australia was a big decision, but it wasn't etched in stone. She could reverse course if warranted.

"No?" Jake asked. "You can't see it that way?"

"What? No. It makes perfect sense."

"Really? You were shaking your head as if you disagreed."

Elizabeth laughed. "I was shaking my head because it's so simple. I don't know why I didn't think of it."

"You're too close to the situation to see it clearly. I'm an outsider, so I have a different perspective."

"Well, thank you for your advice. I'm feeling relieved."

"Keep me around and I'll give you all kinds of good advice."

Elizabeth smiled. Keeping him around was tempting. And not just for his advice. She liked the way he made her feel.

"So are you up for a date?" Jake asked.

"Yes. Just tell me where and when."

"The *when* is easy. How about Saturday night? That is the traditional date night. Unless the babysitters are busy."

"I'll check with my sisters and get back to you."

"Good enough. We have the *when* covered. Now about the *where*."

"I'm easy."

"There are a lot of good places to eat in town," Jake said. "If it's okay with you, I would prefer to avoid the family restaurants and go somewhere a little more upscale."

"It's more than okay. I would prefer an adult-only location," she said.

"In that case, I'll make reservations at Coeur de l'Ouest."

"Ooh-la-la. French name. I take it that's one of Bronco's best?"

"It's the fanciest one in town. I'm sure you'll enjoy it."

"It sounds wonderful. I don't get to dress up often. I miss it."

Jake leaned in close and whispered, "Keep this under your hat, but there are times I actually enjoy wearing a suit and tie."

She pretended to lock her lips. "Your secret is safe with me."

Chapter Nine

"**Y**ou look so pretty, Mummy," Lucy said on Saturday night.

"Thank you." Elizabeth bent over and kissed her daughter's cheek. When she'd packed for this vacation, she'd included two of her favorite dresses even though she hadn't believed she would have the opportunity to wear either of them. Happily she'd been wrong. Tonight she'd had a momentary debate, trying to decide between the little black number that hit her mid-thigh and the red one-shoulder pencil dress. The girls had seen the dresses lying on her bed and immediately cast their votes in favor of the red one.

"I don't know why we can't come on the date," Gianna said, poking out her bottom lip. "We like Jake."

"And he likes you too. But Aunt Faith has brought pizza for you. You're going to have lots of fun."

"Can we have a lamington for dessert?" Lucy asked.

"Yes."

"I guess that's okay," Gianna said slowly.

Elizabeth and Faith exchanged smiles at the twins and their long-suffering attitude. Elizabeth had no doubt the girls would be perfectly content eating their dinner and watching a movie with Faith.

There was a knock on the front door, and her heart skipped a beat. She'd been expecting Jake, so there was no reason her pulse should be racing. No reason she should suddenly be hoping that he liked red.

"I'll get the door," Faith said.

"Thanks," Elizabeth said, taking the opportunity to check her appearance in the mirror before following her sister out of the bedroom.

Faith greeted Jake and welcomed him into the house. His deep voice floated across the air, reaching Elizabeth as she stepped into the main room. She took one look at Jake and smiled. He was attractive in jeans and shirts—even that blindingly bright T-shirt he'd worn the other day—but dressed in a navy suit, light blue shirt and red tie, he was positively dashing.

"Hello," she said, pleased that she'd managed to keep the breathlessness from her voice.

"Hi." Jake crossed the room and placed a kiss on her cheek. The contact was brief and totally appropriate, yet her response was anything but. Her heart skipped a beat and her stomach flip-flopped. Out of nowhere she pictured herself grabbing him by the lapels and laying a hot kiss on him. That was just for starters.

Oblivious to her thoughts, he held out a bouquet of pink roses. "These are for you."

"Thank you."

"Hi, Jake," Gianna said, coming to stand beside him. "Why can't me and Lucy go to dinner with you and Mummy?"

Before Elizabeth could remind Gianna that they had already discussed this, Jake replied. "Because this is an adults-only date. Just like you and Molly have your play-dates. I don't get to come to those."

"But we didn't tell you to stay home," Gianna pointed out. "You can come next time."

Jake chuckled. "Molly might not agree. She likes it being

just you and her. Besides, your mother and I want to talk about grown-up stuff."

"Is Molly going?" Lucy asked.

"No. She's at home with her brothers. Her aunt is baby-sitting them."

"Aunt Faith brought us pizza. And Mummy made lamingtons for dessert."

"What are lamingtons?"

"You don't know what that is?" Gianna asked, her voice soaked with disbelief.

Jake shrugged. "I guess not."

"I'll tell Jake all about them later," Elizabeth said. "We need to get going. Can I have a hug goodbye?"

"Yes," the girls said, rushing over to her.

Elizabeth stooped down and hugged each of her daughters, holding them close before letting them go. To her surprise, they went over to Jake and held out their arms to him. He hesitated for a second, as if touched by their actions, before squatting down and giving them each a tight hug. He rose, a smile on his lips.

"Bye, Mummy. Bye, Jake," the girls said and raced into the kitchen.

"Have fun, you two," Faith said. "Stay out as late as you want. We'll be fine."

"Thanks," Elizabeth said and then turned to Jake. "I'm ready when you are."

He held out his arm, and she took it. Elizabeth had seen Jake's muscles, but even so she was surprised by the strength of his biceps. Tingles shot from her fingers, tripping up her arms to her spine where they danced merrily up and down. It had been years since she'd felt anything remotely like this, and she knew she was in trouble. She'd never been able to separate the physical from the emotional—had never wanted to—and now she was afraid. Sexual attraction was bad enough. Falling in love with Jake could be the worst thing to happen to her right now.

But she was worrying for nothing. Her heart was a long way from getting involved with him.

They stepped outside, and he led her to a sedan. Her confusion must have shown on her face because he smiled and explained. "I don't always drive a truck or SUV. I keep this car in the garage for special occasions. The kids don't ride in it, so it's clean."

He opened the passenger door for her, and she sat down. Once she was settled, he closed her door, circled the vehicle and got inside beside her. His broad shoulders brushed against hers, and the car suddenly felt intimate. She was worried for a bit that things might be awkward between them. After all, this was their first time alone without the kids as a buffer. What if they didn't have anything to talk about?

"Would you like to listen to music?" he asked, his hand hovering over the radio knob.

"I wouldn't mind," Elizabeth said. "So long as it isn't the Wiggles. We saw them in concert last year, and the girls haven't stopped talking about it yet."

"You think that's bad? Wait until they become preteens and discover boy bands. You'll long for these days."

"I take it Molly has reached that age."

"She's only easing into it, so she's not listening to the music nonstop. But I don't know how much longer my luck will hold out. She'll be a teenager soon."

"I remember those years. Being a teenager was so dramatic. Everything was really intense. My feelings were so big." Elizabeth laughed as she recalled her early teen years. "I don't know how my parents survived."

"I can't imagine you being an overwrought teen."

"Believe it." She breathed a sigh of relief as she realized she'd worried about nothing. It was easy being alone with him. She turned in her seat and looked at him, momentarily struck by his strong profile. "I wasn't just moody. I was artistic and moody, which is…shall we say, an interesting combination. I actually sat in my room and wrote some really bad poetry. I even put a couple of them to music and strummed along on my guitar."

He laughed, a rich sound that made goose bumps rise on her arms. Talk about dramatic. Apparently some things hadn't changed with time. "Were these poems about boys?"

"Do you even need to ask? There's something about unrequited love that inspired the creative part of me."

"You wouldn't by chance have recorded any of those songs."

"I did," she said. "But thankfully those recordings no longer exist."

"That's too bad. I would love to hear one. You know, to better understand the kind of music you wrote."

"I don't remember any of the songs, but I can set the mood for you. Picture a girl with long braids dressed in a rainbow T-shirt, cutoff denims, and cowboy boots sitting on her bed. Got it?"

"Yep."

"Now imagine her playing a guitar, singing overwrought and cheesy lyrics featuring words like *broken heart* and *new start*, *crying* and *sighing*. *Pain* and *insane*."

"Please tell me those words weren't part of the actual lyrics." His lips twitched, and she could tell that he was trying to hold back his laughter.

"I was young. And intensely emotional."

"That's a word for it," he said, grinning.

"Don't tell me that you skipped that phase where you felt every emotion deeply. Where you didn't just fall in love, you wallowed in it."

"I thought I hadn't, but now that I know people actually wrote odes about their feelings, I have my doubts. Maybe I missed that part of my development."

"It's not too late," Elizabeth told him. "You can still write poetry."

"I don't think I can rhyme as well as you did."

"There's always free verse."

He gave her a goofy grin. "Has verse been arrested?"

That dad joke was only slightly funny, but Elizabeth couldn't stop the chuckle that burst from her. "That was really terrible. You definitely don't have what it takes to write poetry."

"You're saying I'm not cool enough?"

"And probably not enough angst."

Their laughter mingled.

"How else did you express your emotions?" Jake asked. "Or do I want to know?"

"That was about the most creative. Of course, I did the requisite scribbling of the boy of my dream's name on the cover of my notebook. And practicing writing *Mr. and Mrs.* whoever it was I loved at the time."

"I did the same thing for my crush," Jake said. "I nearly failed world history because instead of taking notes, I was jotting down Sandy's name. Oh, and drawing her portrait."

"So you were an artist?"

"Not really. Hers was the only picture I drew. To be honest, it didn't look a thing like her."

"What happened to Sandy?"

He shrugged. "I have no idea. One day I looked at her

and—poof—the attraction was gone. There was no zing. She went from being special to ordinary overnight."

"I know. What's that about? You go from thinking you'll absolutely die if you don't see that person to looking at them and feeling…nothing."

"Ah, true love ran its course."

Elizabeth nodded. "Funny how that works out."

"Yeah. Until the real thing comes along. Then you know you will never be the same." His voice was wistful and a bit sad.

They reached the restaurant, and Jake pulled up to the valet, exchanged his key for a ticket, and led Elizabeth inside. She looked around. The decor was exquisite. Enormous crystal chandeliers dangled from the high ceiling, casting refracted light around the room. The candlelight flickering on the pristine white tablecloths and over silver cushioned chairs set the perfect ambience.

She smiled. "You weren't kidding when you said this restaurant was fancy. It's positively beautiful."

"This is nothing. Wait until you taste the food. It's even better than the dining room looks."

"I know I'm going to enjoy myself."

Jake gave his name to the maître d', who checked his tablet and then led them through the dining room to a table beside the window. There wasn't a bad table in the restaurant, but Elizabeth was pleased to have a view of the mountains. After sitting in the plush chair, she stared out the window at the snowcapped peaks. There was no denying that Bronco was scenic.

When they'd first arrived in town, the girls had commented on how different the United States looked when compared to Australia. After a week, they'd stopped complaining about the differences, but that didn't mean they'd stopped noticing them. She knew children could be flexible at times, but she didn't want to lean on their ability to adjust any more than necessary. She didn't want to make their lives more difficult than they had to be. For a while she'd feared that was what she'd done by coming to America. But after meeting Jake's kids, Lucy and Gianna seemed so much happier here in Bronco. They were finally making themselves at home, which was a great relief.

"What's good?" Elizabeth asked, turning her mind back to the present.

Jake's brow furrowed. "I suppose I should have mentioned this before. They have a fixed menu."

"Oh."

"I hope that's okay."

"It's fine," she said and then smiled. "That takes away some of the decisions."

"I take it that you're tired of making those."

"You could say that."

"The server has a menu with tonight's meal if you want to look at it."

She shook her head. "No. I love surprises. I'll look at this as adventure eating." The aromas filling the air were tantalizing, and she knew she would enjoy whatever was served.

"You are so easygoing. I love that about you." His mouth fell open as if he realized what he'd said. A hint of panic surrounded him as if he feared that she might take his words out of context. He needn't have worried. She understood what he meant.

"Right back at you," she said, injecting her words with lightness, hoping to put him at ease again. This was too nice a night to ruin. She might not be looking for love, but she wasn't immune to his appeal—and he had appeal to spare. It was everything from his gorgeous face to his well-defined chest to his muscular thighs. Suddenly she felt warm all over. She lifted her glass of ice water and took a long sip. The water was cold enough to make her teeth chatter, but it did little to douse the flames inside her. Her mind might know that she wasn't interested in a romance, but her body was rejecting the message.

Elizabeth leaned her chin into her palm and looked at Jake. "Tell me more about yourself."

"What do you want to know?"

"Whatever you want to tell me. You told me your parents live in town now. Did you grow up in Bronco or move here later? What do you like about the town? What do you like about being a rancher? Give me your best sales pitch."

He laughed, and the sound made her stomach do a ridiculous little flip-flop. "So you want me to sell you on Bronco."

She shrugged. "I'm looking to add to my knowledge so I can make an informed decision. I've lived in Australia for a decade, so I know pretty much everything I need to know about Queensland. But it's been a while since I've lived in America. And I've never lived in Bronco. All told, I don't think I spent more than a week in Montana, so my knowledge is limited."

He rubbed his hands together and grinned. "Then sit back and prepare to be wowed."

"I'm all ears," she said and then laughed when she recalled Pete's bad joke. Clearly father and son shared the same sense of humor.

"Let me answer your first question. I did grow up in Bronco Valley."

"I keep hearing people talk about Bronco Heights or Valley, but I'm not sure what the difference is. Maybe you can explain it to me."

He tapped his fingertips together and her eyes were immediately drawn to his long, lean fingers. They were tanned and she noticed a couple of nicks on his knuckles. Suddenly she imagined his fingers caressing her body.

"Bronco is really two towns," he explained, pulling her attention back to his words. "Bronco Heights is where the wealthier people live. You know, big houses on big lots. Bronco Valley is home to the middle class. There may be a big difference in bank accounts, but the people in the Valley and the Heights generally get along well together."

"So there aren't cliques."

"I didn't say that. People may associate with some of their neighbors and not others. They have their friend groups. But those groups aren't defined by wealth or neighborhood. Nor are they opposed to other groups. They're based on shared interests."

She nodded slowly. "That's good to know."

"Is that a plus for the town?"

"If I'm keeping score, then yes," she said. "But it's the same way back home, so that doesn't give Bronco an edge."

He rubbed his chin. "Oh. You're a tough sell."

"Surely you want to earn your win. You don't want me to just give it to you, do you?"

"I don't know who told you that. I'll take victory any way I can get it."

"So, no oversize male ego for you?"

"I have three children. Two of them are boys. They make fun of me like it's their job. It's hilarious to them. In case you haven't noticed, they're brutal. They don't hold anything back. If I didn't have thick skin, I'd be in tears every day. You can't have an ego of any size and be a parent of boys."

Elizabeth laughed. "That is so true. Even with girls. Gianna and Lucy love me with their whole hearts, but they are still at an age when they haven't learned diplomacy. Trust me, I know when my hairstyle doesn't *accentuate the positives*, should I say. And I know when I've eaten too many onions because my breath stinks."

He laughed with her and then continued, "Back to my sales pitch. You already know about the restaurants that we have."

"Yes. I've eaten at a couple. They were good."

"I don't suppose I'll get points for mentioning the rodeos we have."

"Considering that my family competes in them and that I might as well?" She shrugged. "Maybe. It has been quite a while since I've seen my sisters and cousins compete. It would be interesting to participate with them."

"Oh. An unexpected point," he said, one side of his mouth lifting in a sexy grin. "I'll take that."

She held up a finger to stop him from gloating. "Of course, Carly and I often compete in the same rodeos back home, so there is no advantage here."

"Sure there is. You only have one sister in Queensland, but you have three sisters and several cousins here. Bronco has numbers."

She nodded. "I'll give you that one."

The server brought their meals, and they stopped talking long enough to sample everything. Elizabeth closed her eyes, and a hum slipped through her lips.

"Well?" Jake asked.

She opened her eyes and looked directly at him. "You already know the answer. It is absolutely delicious. Probably the best thing I've ever eaten in my life."

"Another point for Bronco."

"Oh, yes. I wasn't even thinking of that."

"You might not be keeping score, but I am."

Elizabeth laughed. Although she would never admit it, Jake's presence was a point in Bronco's favor. No man in Australia appealed to her, and she didn't expect one ever would. Of course, she hadn't expected to meet anyone here either. Despite her intentions to avoid romantic entanglements, she was drawn to Jake. The feeling of disloyalty was fading, but it wasn't entirely gone. It still had a hold on her emotions, although it was losing its grip. At some point she would have to overcome that feeling, whether or not she and Jake decided to have a relationship. If only she knew the way to get rid of it.

"I'll keep that in mind," she said.

As they ate, they talked about everything under the sun. Jake was quite amusing, even with his corny dad jokes, and Elizabeth laughed more than she had in years. He regaled her with stories of growing up with a sister. They had been good friends even back then, but often had blowout disagreements. Luckily neither of them held a grudge and they had maintained their closeness.

The meal was spectacular, and each bite was even tastier than the one that preceded it. The flavors were layered and complemented each other. Although Elizabeth wasn't much of a foodie, she appreciated the way each course had been designed to build upon the previous ones. But as magnificent as the meal was, it came in a distant second to Jake.

When the server set the dessert in front of her, Elizabeth sighed. "I can't believe this delicious dinner is coming to an end."

"It has been good."

Elizabeth tasted her cake. "This is so good. A fitting end to a wonderful meal."

"Speaking of dessert. What is a lamington?"

"It's one of the most popular Australian desserts. Basically it's a little bit of heaven."

"Can you bring it down to earth for those of us who haven't been to Australia to enjoy one?"

"Yes. Sorry. It's a square of sponge cake coated in chocolate sauce and rolled in coconut. The girls love them. It can be a bit messy to make, but it's worth it."

"It sounds good."

"It's better than good. I'll make some for you and the kids. Then you'll be hooked."

He nodded. "I can get with that."

"You've cooked for me and the girls a couple of times. How about I make an authentic Australian meal for you and your kids?"

"I think they'll love it. I know I will."

"When is a good time?" she asked.

"As soon as you want. Tomorrow. The next day. We eat dinner all the time. Practically every day."

She rolled her eyes. His dad jokes had gotten worse throughout the meal, yet they amused her to no end.

"Do you want us to come out to the cabin, or would you rather use my kitchen? That way the twins could play on the swings and in the tree house."

"That would be nice. Your kitchen is bigger and your table seats more people. We'll be more comfortable there."

"Then it's a date. How about Monday?"

She nodded. "That sounds good."

They finished their dessert, and Jake paid the bill. "Are you up for a walk before we head back to the cabin? It's such a nice night."

She nodded. "I'm enjoying myself immensely, so yes."

The night was slightly cool but still pleasant. There were very few streetlights out this way, and the darkness cloaked them in intimacy. Elizabeth paused, then turned in a slow circle. "I love looking at the sky here. It's so deep and dark. The moon and stars seem so much brighter."

"One more point for Bronco," Jake said.

"I can't believe you're still keeping score."

"I told you, I'm in it to win it."

"You're determined, I'll give you that."

"When the prize is getting you to stay in town, most definitely."

Elizabeth's heart skipped a beat. It had been a while since a man had gone out of his way to win her over. Jake was definitely giving it his all.

He reached out and took her hand into his. His palm was calloused, evidence of hard work, but his touch was gentle. Electricity shot from her fingers throughout her body. Goose bumps popped up on her arms and she shivered.

"Cold?" Jake asked. Before she could answer, he released her hand and draped his arm around her shoulder. He pulled her close and the warmth from his body wrapped around hers.

Elizabeth drew in a breath, inhaling his intoxicating scent. Coherent thought fled and it was all she could do to put one foot in front of the other without stumbling.

They walked in silence for a few more minutes before they returned to the car. The ride to the cabin was relaxing, and they chatted companionably. As they got closer to the cabin, Elizabeth's anticipation grew. Her nerves jangled, and she wondered how the night would end. How would they say good-night? Would he kiss her?

Her desires were wreaking havoc on her emotions. She hadn't kissed a man other than Arlo since their first date nearly a decade ago. She hadn't wanted to. Now she was actually contemplating it. More than that, she wanted it.

Elizabeth was ready to admit that her attraction was

more than physical. It was becoming emotional. Surprisingly, the admission came with only a small side of guilt. That was a step in the right direction. Another step and she'd consider the possibility of falling in love.

Not that she had decided that Jake was that man. There were so many things she needed to figure out, not the least of which was where she and the girls were going to live.

She looked up and realized that Jake was pulling up to the cabin. He turned off the engine. Instead of getting out of the car, he glanced over at her, a slight smile tugging on his lips. His eyes were filled with mischief. "So."

She looked back at him, waiting for him to say more. When he didn't, she echoed him. "So."

"I had a really great time."

"So did I."

"Good enough to do it again?"

"You mean go to dinner at Coeur de l'Ouest?" She knew that wasn't what he meant, but she needed a minute to gather her feelings.

He chuckled. "We can do that again, sure. But that's not exactly what I meant. I was talking about going on a date again."

"Are you talking about dating? Or going on a date?"

"I hadn't thought about it like that. But…I'd say dating. How do you feel about that?"

"I like the idea." Had she actually just said that? The answer had burst from her before she'd had the opportunity to mull it over. Perhaps that was for the best. After all, Jake had asked how she *felt*, not what she *thought*. She had enough going on in her brain without trying to crowd in more. Maybe going with her feelings was best in this instance.

"So do I." He nodded and then opened his door.

That was it? She wasn't certain of the kind of reaction she had been expecting, but that wasn't it.

He opened her door and held out his hand, helping her to get out. She took his hand, and sparks flared at the contact and her anticipation grew. Though her reaction was ridiculous, she had to admit that she liked the sensation. Jake was a man worthy of her attraction. He was a good father to his kids and was kind to her daughters. He showed Gianna and Lucy the same patience and concern he gave his children, yet somehow he managed not to overstep. That was a tight line to walk, and he traveled it quite well.

They reached the cabin and paused. The breeze blew, shaking the leaves on the trees and rattling the wind chimes. She inhaled, and her lungs were filled with the sweet fragrance of flowers. With a sky full of stars, the setting was incredibly romantic. The perfect place for a first kiss. She wanted it. Did Jake?

"I'm not exactly sure what to do now," Jake said, his soft voice breaking into her musing.

"Neither am I," she admitted.

"I want to kiss you, Elizabeth. But I'm worried about… well…messing up things between us."

His confession chased away her nervousness. The tension in her body vanished, and she relaxed. "There's only one way to find out."

A cocky grin flashed across his face a second before he reached out and pulled her into his arms. His head lowered and he pressed his lips against hers in a searing kiss. The electric shock that she'd experienced when they'd held hands was nothing compared to this. It was as if she'd touched a live wire with wet hands. Her entire body tingled from the top of her head to the toes of her feet. Even her hair seemed to vibrate with excitement. Being held against his hard, muscular body felt like heaven.

He deepened the kiss, and she opened her mouth to him. As he swept his tongue inside, her pleasure multiplied. Multiplied again. Elizabeth closed her eyes, allowing herself to enjoy sensations that she hadn't experienced in years. She knew she should pull back—this was a first kiss after all—but the feelings rocketing through her body felt too good and she didn't want to stop. And as Jake didn't seem inclined to end the kiss either, it went on and on.

Finally her mind regained control of her emotions, and she pulled back. Kissing Jake had felt so good. She knew it would be easy to let the fire burning inside her turn into a raging inferno, sweeping her away.

But could that lead her even closer to the kind of complication she wanted to avoid?

Chapter Ten

Jake felt Elizabeth easing away and forced himself to release her, reluctantly ending the kiss. It had been forever since he'd held a woman in his arms, an eternity since he'd experienced pleasure this intense. Despite the years that had passed, he still recognized when a woman wanted to slow things down. Though he was loath to admit it, that was a good plan for now. This was their first kiss. He hoped it wasn't their last—he would be ready for the second one to start soon—but he knew they needed to keep their wits about them. After all, there were other people to consider. Their children had each lost a parent. If he and Elizabeth decided to pursue a relationship, they needed to be sure that it would last so their kids didn't get hurt. They had to be sure they were making wise decisions. Thinking clearly would be harder to do under the haze of lust.

Leaning his forehead against hers, Jake breathed out a long sigh. There was no reason to hide his feelings. They were probably obvious to Elizabeth. "That was some kiss."

"Yes it was." Although her face was hidden in the shadows, he heard the smile in her voice. That husky tone made him want to pull her back into his arms for their second kiss, but he resisted. Hopefully there would be time for that again in the near future.

"So." He dragged the word out over several syllables. "I suppose we should say good-night now."

She nodded and unlocked the front door. She stepped inside and then turned and looked at him. "Coming in?"

It was tempting. "I'd better get going. Bethany is waiting up for me."

"Okay."

"I'll call you tomorrow."

"I'll look forward to it."

Jake waited until Elizabeth closed the door behind her before getting into his car and driving away. Thankfully traffic was light, and he made good time. As he drove, he replayed the date in his mind, recalling every detail. Every move Elizabeth made, every smile she turned in his direction was etched in his memory. The sound of her laughter had illuminated the dark spot in his heart that had developed over the years. As the night had progressed, he realized that spot had faded into nothingness.

Just looking at her had been pure joy. Her red dress had fit her body so perfectly it must have been made for her. It had clung to her body, caressing her curves and leaving nothing to the imagination. In her heels, her shapely legs seemed to go on forever. Jake didn't like to use the word *perfect* to describe a person because he knew that everyone had flaws. Even so, Elizabeth was as close to perfect as a person could get.

Although he generally drove in silence, he'd left on the radio. A pop song he remembered from his high school days started to play, and he hummed along. That song was followed by another familiar one. He turned up the volume and tapped the beat on the steering wheel. By the time he pulled into the garage and got out of the car, he was singing. When he realized what he was doing, he nearly tripped.

He couldn't recall the last time he'd hummed, much less sung. Apparently Elizabeth brought music back to his life.

His singing turned into laughter, echoing around the vast backyard. That had to be the corniest thing he'd ever thought. Yet it was true. Elizabeth made him so happy that he was singing out loud.

He unlocked the back door and stepped inside. It was way past the kids' bedtime, but that never mattered to Bethany. Whenever she babysat, she let them stay up as long as they wanted, which meant he usually found them sprawled on the living room floor, fighting sleep.

Jake was surprised to find Bethany alone on the couch, reading a mystery. The television was on, but the volume was turned down so low she couldn't possibly hear it.

"Hey," she said, looking up. She used a bookmark to save her place and then set the book on the table beside her. "How was your date? Tell me everything."

He inhaled and then smiled. He and Bethany hadn't talked about their dates since they were in their teens. For him, there hadn't been much to talk about until he and Maggie had started going out. "I'm kind of beat. I think I'd rather go right to bed."

"Really?" She sounded disappointed.

He couldn't keep a straight face any longer and felt himself grinning. "No way. I find myself in a talkative mood."

She picked up her paperback and tossed it in his direction. Laughing, he caught it and set it on the coffee table.

"You know I'm going to pay you back for that, Jake."

"When I least expect it, I'll expect it," he said, parroting the familiar threat they said to each other as kids. Of course, they'd very rarely followed up on it. "Where are the kids?"

"In bed asleep, where they've been since bedtime."

"Really? Generally you ignore that rule."

She shrugged. "I had a bit of a headache and needed some quiet."

"Why didn't you say something? How are you feeling now? Can I get you an aspirin?" He leaned in closer and studied her. "You do look a little green around the gills."

"I was a little queasy, but I'm fine now. And don't try to change the subject." She patted the cushion next to her. "Sit down and tell me everything."

"Are you sure you don't need some ginger ale or maybe some tea?"

She picked up a glass from the table beside her, then gestured to the half-eaten sleeve of saltines. "I have everything I need. Tell me about your date. And don't leave out a single detail."

"In that case…" He sat down and cleared his throat dramatically. "I had a great time. Dinner was perfect. The restaurant had wonderful ambiance. The view was second to none. The food was delicious, and the service was impeccable."

"I see." Bethany smiled and then turned in her seat so that she was looking at him. "Okay. Now get to the juicy parts. Did you kiss her good-night?"

"Are you kidding me? You want to jump to the end of the evening? Don't you want to know what we talked about?"

"Later. But first…" She wound her hand in a circle. "The kiss?"

He felt himself smiling as he remembered the sensation that had rocketed through him as their lips had touched. Describing the feeling as *electric* was underselling it by half. But he didn't have a good enough vocabulary to do it justice. Even an hour later his lips still tingled as if every nerve ending had been turned up to eleven. Nothing had ever felt as good. He couldn't wait to do it again.

"From the look on your face I'm going to go out on a limb and say the kiss was good."

"Better than good. It was like nothing of this world." He heaved out a sigh. "I don't know how to describe it to you."

She laughed and held her hands out in front of her as if trying to stop the words from coming out of his mouth. "That's okay. I want details, but not *those* details. Just knowing that she rocked your world is enough."

"Are you sure? Because I can be more specific," he said. When Bethany covered her ears and began to hum, Jake laughed. "I guess you don't want the blow-by-blow."

"Let's rewind back to the beginning of the date. What was Elizabeth wearing?"

He closed his eyes, and Elizabeth's image appeared in front of him. Beads of sweat popped out on his brow as his temperature rose at the memory. "She had on a red dress that fit her like a second skin. Well, maybe not that tight, but it was really sexy."

"I get the picture. She looked good."

"Let's just say that red is now my favorite color."

She shook her head and laughed. "You are so predictable."

"I get the feeling that's not good."

"It is good," Bethany said quickly. "I just bet that whatever color she wears on your next date will become your new favorite color."

"I fail to see the problem with that."

"There isn't one." Her smile faded and her expression grew serious. "It does my heart good to see you this way."

"What way?"

"Happy. Playful. You always put on a good front for the kids, but I still can see the sadness in you. It's diminished over the years, but there was always a hint of it. Like a shadow. No, like a ghost hovering around you. It's not here tonight. You seem truly happy."

"I am." Jake heard his words and realized he was telling the truth. He actually felt happy inside. The smile wasn't for Bethany. He wasn't being jolly in order to keep the kids happy. He wasn't faking it until he could make it. He had made it to the other side of his grieving. It had taken a while, maybe longer than it should have, but he was healed. More than that, he was ready to take a chance on love again.

"How was tonight?" Faith asked. She handed Elizabeth a glass of lemonade and then took a sip of her own.

Elizabeth leaned against the back of the sofa and placed her bare feet on the coffee table. She'd washed her face, brushed her hair, and changed into a pair of shorts and a T-shirt. She was completely relaxed and eager to relive the date with Faith. No doubt Tori and Amy would expect a recap tomorrow. She'd enjoyed herself so much that she relished the idea of talking about tonight as many times as possible.

"It was wonderful," Elizabeth said with a contented sigh. "It was the most fun I've had in years. Pure bliss."

"Pure bliss, eh?" her sister looked at her. "Tell me every-thing. Don't leave out a single thing."

Elizabeth launched into a detailed retelling of the eve-ning. Faith nodded every now and again, but instead of it being a dialogue, it was more of a monologue.

"What do you think?" Elizabeth asked after she'd told her sister about everything, including that hot kiss. *Espe-cially* that hot kiss.

"I think you sound happier than you have in years."

"But?" Although Faith hadn't said anything negative, Elizabeth sensed her sister had more to say. Faith generally spoke her mind, so this reticence was a surprise. "Don't feel like you have to hold back. I'm not fragile any longer. I won't break if you tell me what you're thinking."

"I'm not the right person to ask about romance. At least not now."

"Why? What's going on now?"

Faith sighed. "I'm not in the best frame of mind when it comes to relationships. I don't have a lot of warm feelings for men these days."

Elizabeth nodded. "I know things haven't worked out for you in the past. But I still believe there's a wonderful man waiting for you. He's probably just around the corner."

"You always were the optimist. I can't believe that after all you've been through that you still have that kind of faith and willingness to put yourself out there."

"Hold on. I think we're talking about two different things. I was hurt after Arlo died, but that didn't make me stop trusting men. My relationship with Arlo was the best thing that happened to me. Losing him was devastating. My reluctance to get involved has nothing to do with thinking someone will break my heart."

"I know. I like Jake. He seems like the real deal."

"I think so too. And I have a feeling that sooner rather than later the right man for you is going to come along and you're going to fall head over heels for him. He'll feel the same way about you."

Faith scoffed. "I'm not sure if that's a blessing or a curse. I thought you loved me."

"You know I love you. You also know I only want the best for you. And just to be clear, that was a blessing."

"Then I'll take your words in the spirit they were intended."

"Thank you."

Faith stood. "And on that note, I'm going to head home."

"You know you're welcome to stay the night here."

"I know, but I'll pass. It would be a bit tight."

"We could have a sleepover like we did in the old days. Those were always fun."

Faith laughed. "With you talking my ears off? I wouldn't get a bit of sleep all night."

"Probably not," Elizabeth admitted.

"Unlike when we were kids, I need my sleep."

"All right. If you're going to be all adult about it. Text me when you get home."

"Will do."

They walked to the door together. Elizabeth opened it and then turned to her sister. "Thanks again for watching the girls for me. I appreciate it."

Faith took her hand and gave it a squeeze. "It was my pleasure. I love every minute I get to spend with my nieces."

Elizabeth smiled. "I'm glad you're all getting to know each other."

Faith got into her car, waved, and then drove away. Once she could no longer see the taillights on her sister's car, Elizabeth closed the door and went to check on the girls. As usual, Gianna's thin blanket was twisted around her legs. Elizabeth straightened it and then brushed a kiss on her daughter's forehead. Lucy was half-in and half-out of her bed, so Elizabeth lifted her and placed her on the middle of the mattress. She kissed Lucy's forehead and then tiptoed from the room, closing the door behind her.

When she was in her own room, Elizabeth changed into her favorite cotton pajamas and hopped into the bed. She doubted that Jake would be sleeping, and before she could talk herself out of it, she grabbed her phone and shot off a quick text to him.

Just checking to see if you made it home okay.

That wasn't entirely true, but he didn't need to know that she couldn't stop thinking about him. Couldn't stop wishing she could be in his arms right now.

Jake's reply came immediately.

Yep. I've been here for a while. I'm waiting for my sister to text that she got home. I tried to get her to stay the night, but she preferred to sleep in her own bed.

Elizabeth read his text and smiled before she replied.

I'm glad I didn't wake you.

She wasn't sure what else to say. She hadn't reached out with any particular topic in mind. She'd just wanted to get in touch with him. No, it was more than that. She actually wanted to hear his voice. Her phone dinged, signaling a new text.

Do you feel like talking? That would be a lot better than texting.

She smiled, relieved they were on the same wavelength.

That sounds great.

A few seconds later her mobile phone rang, and she answered it before it could ring a second time.

"Jake?" Her voice sounded breathless, as if she'd been running as opposed to sitting in her bed.

"It's good to hear your voice. I was tempted to call you, but I didn't want to risk waking you up."

"I'm normally asleep at this time," she admitted, "but not tonight. Like you, I'm waiting for my sister to let me know when she's home."

There was a brief silence, but it wasn't uncomfortable. In fact, it was quite relaxing. It was nice not to feel compelled to fill the silence with conversation. Though they were in their separate homes she still felt connected with him.

Elizabeth often missed the activity and the excitement of being with Arlo. With the girls around, she was able to keep busy. Filling her day with activity kept the loneliness at bay. But in the quiet of the night when the girls were asleep, Elizabeth was alone with her thoughts. For a while she'd been consumed with sadness. Eventually that sorrow had faded into melancholy. Now even that was gone, leaving behind acceptance.

Tonight she was filled with contentment. Perhaps because she was sharing the night with Jake.

After a while they began to talk again. They didn't speak about anything of consequence, but they didn't need to. Keeping the connection alive was the important thing.

They talked for about twenty minutes before Jake sighed. "I suppose I should let you go to sleep. Would it be okay if I called you in the morning?"

"Of course. Are you still bringing Molly over tomorrow?"

"Yes. But I thought we could talk before then. That is, if you don't mind."

"I don't mind at all." She actually relished the idea of starting her day with an adult conversation. "Especially since I'll get to talk to you again."

"Then I'll talk to you in the morning."

After they said good-night, Elizabeth held her phone. Their relationship had shifted tonight.

She just hoped that she was ready for the changes that shift would bring.

Chapter Eleven

Elizabeth grabbed the bags of groceries from the back seat, then headed for the steps. "Come on, girls."

"Why can't we just go in the backyard and get on the swings?" Gianna asked, looking over her shoulder. She was halfway between the car and the side of the house.

Lucy, standing beside her sister, nodded. "We want to play."

"Because we need to say hello first. We don't just go into someone's backyard and start playing. That's rude."

"But that's where everybody is," Gianna said. "Can't you hear them?"

Elizabeth nodded. The wind carried the children's laughter over to them. She knew Molly, Pete, and Ben would be glad to see the twins and would immediately welcome them into their game. They'd spent a lot of time together and now treated each other like old friends. Dare she say like family? Should she insist on standing on formality? Clearly her girls felt at home here.

"Fine, go on back. But be careful. And say hello before you start playing."

Those last words had been spoken to the air because the girls had run away the minute Elizabeth had given her approval. Shaking her head, Elizabeth climbed the stairs. Before she could ring the doorbell, she heard her name being called.

"Let me help you with that," Jake said, jogging around the porch and up the stairs.

"Thanks." Elizabeth handed over two of the three bags she'd been carrying.

"Am I holding the secret ingredients for an authentic Australian dinner?"

"I don't know how secret they are. I'm making some of the most popular foods from home, and the recipes are available everywhere. The girls were supposed to help me carry everything, but they abandoned me the second we got here."

"They love the swings. They hopped on the minute they stepped into the yard."

She shook her head. "I told them to say hello first."

Jake shrugged as they walked into the kitchen. "They did. All in one smooth motion."

"I suppose that's something."

"They're kids." He set the bag on the table and then pulled aside the curtain. "Look. They're having a great time."

Elizabeth set down her bag, then glanced through the window. Gianna and Ben were swinging and laughing as each tried to go higher than the other. Lucy was standing at the top of the ladder, waiting for Pete to slide so she could have her turn.

"Where's Molly?" Elizabeth asked.

"She was out there a minute ago."

The back door opened with a crash. Molly burst into the room. She was breathing hard as if she had just run across the enormous yard.

"Hi, Elizabeth. I didn't know you were here yet."

She turned and smiled at Molly. "We just got here."

"Daddy said you're going to cook some real Australian food for us. Can I help?"

"That would be wonderful."

"I can't wait to eat Australian food. All Daddy ever makes is boring regular food."

Jake laughed, clearly not at all bothered by having his food be dissed so spectacularly. But then, hadn't he already admitted that his kids were brutally honest, emphasis on *brutal*? "That's the only kind of food I know how to make."

"You should get some cookbooks so you can learn to make new foods," Molly said to him before turning back to Elizabeth, who managed to keep her amusement from showing on her face. "I told him that before, but he didn't listen to me."

"The food we'll be cooking is easy to make. But it's delicious. If everyone likes it, I'll write down the recipes so you can make it anytime you want."

"I know we're going to like it. We liked the biscuits a lot."

Elizabeth smiled at Molly's use of the Australian term. "Let's wash our hands and get started."

Molly and Elizabeth washed their hands at the kitchen sink. They stepped aside when they were finished, and Jake grabbed the soap.

Molly was wiping her hands on a paper towel. She stopped and looked at her father. "Why are you washing your hands? Elizabeth and I are the ones who are going to cook. Not you."

A look of disappointment flashed across his face before it was replaced by a smile that didn't quite reach his eyes. "I thought I might stick around and help. That way I will know how to make it later."

"Elizabeth said she would write it down. Plus, I'll know how to make it."

"Molly, you might not always want to cook," Elizabeth said. She didn't want this to turn into a battle. The day was supposed to be fun. More than that, it hurt her heart to see Jake so disappointed. Elizabeth knew Molly didn't mean to be cruel. She loved her father too much to deliberately hurt him. She just had her own idea of how the day should go. "It will be good if your father knows how to cook these dishes too."

Molly frowned, clearly not happy with the turn of events. Jake could read her feelings too. "How about I go see what the others are doing?" he asked. "If you need my help, you can just call me."

"Okay. Bye," Molly said.

Elizabeth gave him a smile. Even though she had been looking forward to Jake's company, if he was giving his daughter this opportunity to learn how to make these dishes without him, Elizabeth certainly wasn't going to get in the way. Besides, she empathized with Molly. She probably didn't get many opportunities to have time alone with a woman. Elizabeth would never try to replace Molly's mother, but she could help when she could.

Molly watched her father walk out the door and then turned back to Elizabeth. Her face was glowing with excitement. "What are we making?"

"We're going to make meat pies, peas, and mashed potatoes. For dessert we'll make Pavlova. How does that sound?"

"What kind of pie has meat in it?"

"Only the best kind."

"What's a Pavlova?"

Elizabeth dug her mobile from her purse and went to one of her favorite food blogs. When she found a good image, she handed the phone to Molly. "This is a picture of a Pavlova. Isn't it pretty?"

Molly's brow wrinkled. "That looks really hard to make. Maybe we need Daddy's help after all."

"No way," Elizabeth said. "It looks hard but it's easy. Trust me, okay?"

Molly thought for a moment. Then her face cleared up and she smiled. "Okay. I trust you."

Elizabeth showed Molly how to cube the beef. When they were done, Elizabeth put the meat in a pot to brown. Then they moved on to the next step.

As they worked, Molly peppered Elizabeth with questions.

"Am I cutting the onions right?" she asked.

"You're doing a great job."

"I wish they didn't make me cry so much."

"I can do them," Elizabeth offered.

Molly shook her head. "I want to do it."

"Rinse your hands. That should help."

Molly washed her hands and rinsed her eyes. She grabbed the knife and began to work again. "I want to be a good cook like you."

Elizabeth didn't point out that Molly hadn't eaten much of her cooking. Maybe in her mind all mothers were good cooks. "You're off to a great start."

"Do you think I'm too young to have a pink streak in my hair?"

Where had that come from? The question was too off-topic to be a spur-of-the-moment query. Perhaps Molly had already asked Jake and he had said no. Elizabeth didn't know. One thing was certain—she wasn't going to get drawn into the middle of a parent-and-child dispute. "I don't know. What does your father say?"

"I didn't ask him. He doesn't know anything about hair. Not like you do. Just look at the way he wears his. It's all boring."

Elizabeth thought Jake had attractive hair. His haircut could be described as *traditional* but never as *boring*. But then, Elizabeth didn't want to put a pink streak in her hair either. Maybe in Molly's eyes Elizabeth's hair was boring too. "Do you want a pink streak?"

"Maybe. Sometimes. I saw this girl on TV with a blue streak. But blue is for boys."

"How old was the girl?"

"Maybe fourteen or fifteen."

"I suppose that might be the right age, then," Elizabeth said, taking the coward's way out. But really, she didn't know what was considered appropriate in Montana. She didn't want to set up Molly for ridicule. Or worse, judgment.

Elizabeth had never been conservative. She believed people should do what made them happy as long as their actions didn't hurt anyone else. If she was Molly's mother, she would let her dye her hair any color she wanted. Heck, she'd take her to the salon and have it done professionally. But that was *her*. When she recalled Jake's reaction to Molly's manicure, she had a feeling he wasn't the type to approve of a pink streak.

"You're probably right," Molly said.

As they worked, Elizabeth marveled at Molly's focus. She was determined to do everything exactly as Elizabeth instructed. Every once in a while, she would pause to let Elizabeth check her work, holding her breath all the while. Elizabeth made a point of praising Molly even when she corrected her.

Molly jumped from one topic to another. She asked Elizabeth's opinion on everything from music to TV shows to books. When Elizabeth replied, Molly nodded as if storing Elizabeth's words in her mind, planning to make them her own in the future. As a mother, Elizabeth knew she had a big influence on her daughters. They parroted her words back to her on occasion. More than once, she'd heard them addressing their dolls in the same tone and using the same words as she used with them.

It was clear that she had the same influence on Molly. She wasn't entirely comfortable with that knowledge. She wasn't Molly's parent or even her stepparent. Should she have that type of impact on Molly's thinking? She wasn't sure. But since she'd stepped on the proverbial landmine in the past, she would be more cautious this time. She would talk to Jake and let him decide how she should proceed.

Once the beef was simmering and the tables and counters were wiped, Elizabeth turned to Molly. "This is going to take a while, so we need to start on the Pavlova."

"Are you sure it won't be hard to make?"

"Positive. But it's important that we follow the directions carefully. We'll need egg whites for the meringue, but it's important that not even one bit of yolk gets in. Otherwise it won't fluff up."

"Maybe you should do that part."

"No way. We're a team. We can do it together." Elizabeth showed Molly how to carefully separate the whites from the yolks, then they worked together to complete the task.

"Your dad can scramble the yolks for breakfast tomorrow," Elizabeth said, sealing them in a container.

"Okay," Molly said. "I'll tell him."

When the egg whites reached room temperature, they added sugar and beat them. When the meringue was finished, they set it in a preheated oven.

"This is where we need a little luck," Elizabeth said.

"Why?"

"Because if there's a lot of noise and bumping in the kitchen, it might fall. It will still taste good. It just won't be as pretty."

"We shouldn't let anyone come in the house, then," Molly said.

"That's a bit extreme. They might need to go to the bathroom. We'll just ask them to tiptoe. When it's done, we'll let it cool in the oven. I'll keep watch on it while we're outside so you don't have to worry about that."

"Okay."

"Now let's go outside. The girls have been looking forward to playing with you. I can talk to your dad for a while."

"You won't do anything without me, will you?" Molly asked.

"No. I may come in every thirty minutes or so to stir the meat, but that's it. When it's time to do anything else, I'll let you know."

Molly grinned. She took two steps, then paused. Then she ran over and gave Elizabeth a quick hug before running out the door. Elizabeth stood frozen as unexpected emotions coursed through her. She hadn't expected to feel this strongly for Molly. Not that she didn't want to care for the little girl. Of course she did. But Elizabeth couldn't put herself in the position of being a surrogate mother when she wasn't sure how long she would be in Molly's life. Judging by Molly's behavior, that ship might have sailed.

Elizabeth and Jake's relationship was still in its infancy. It might not progress any further than it had. Elizabeth didn't know everything about romance, but she knew that one hot kiss didn't a relationship make.

Despite all that, this turn of events wasn't necessarily bad. Elizabeth had plenty of room in her heart, plenty of love to give to a motherless child or three. Giving and receiving love was never a bad thing.

Elizabeth stepped outside and looked around. She'd expected Jake to be sitting on the patio, but he was playing in the yard with the kids. He was pushing Gianna on a swing while watching Lucy do her version of a cartwheel across the grass.

"That's good, Lucy," he called when she stopped and looked at him. "You're a great tumbler."

"Thank you," she said, then launched into another one.

"Look at me, Daddy," Ben yelled, standing on the top of the slide. "I can go upside down."

"I'm watching."

Ben grinned and then slid headfirst. His hands shot out and hit the ground a half second before his head would have slammed onto the grass. He sat up, then grinned at Jake, who gave him a thumbs-up.

Molly was standing beside Jake and talking a mile a minute. No doubt she was telling him all about her adventures in cooking. The only person who wasn't trying to attract Jake's attention was Pete, who was tossing a ball into the air and catching it in his glove.

Jake looked over at Elizabeth and smiled before turning his attention back to the kids. She didn't know how he did it. He seemed so relaxed and at ease, as if dividing his attention between all these kids at once was second nature. There were times when she felt overwhelmed just dealing with two.

Since Jake had everything under control, she decided to take a few minutes to herself and sat down on the patio. After a while, Molly sat on a swing beside Gianna and Ben grabbed a glove and began to play catch with Pete.

Jake took a look around, ambled over to the patio, and sat next to Elizabeth.

"You have skills," she said.

"What skills might those be? The way I sat down? Clearly I'm the boss of the chair."

Elizabeth giggled and punched him in the shoulder. "I was talking about the way you handled the kids. They were all over the place, but you managed to give all of them attention. How did you do it?"

"I'm used to it. Pete was on his own, and up until a few minutes ago you had Molly."

"I guess that's fair."

"Molly said she had a lot of fun with you. She also told me that you're a much better cook than I am."

Elizabeth laughed. "I hope she feels that way after we eat."

"Trust me, you can do no wrong in her eyes. She's very fond of you."

Elizabeth smiled. "The feeling goes both ways."

Ben and Pete called for Jake to join their game of catch.

"Do you want to play?" Jake asked Elizabeth.

"Sure. But be warned, I haven't thrown a ball in years."

"It's like riding a bike."

"No, I don't think it is. You use your legs for one and your hands for another."

"You're cute," Jake said. "I meant it's not something you forget how to do."

"I would love to join the game. That is if the boys don't mind."

"That's not going to ever be a problem. My boys think you're the best. And so do I."

Her heart skipped a beat, and she smiled. She was coming to think the same about all of them.

"Are you going to play ball, Elizabeth?" Molly called from her swing.

"I'm going to try."

Pete and Ben cheered and instantly claimed her for their team.

"I want to play," Molly said, running over.

"Me too," Gianna said, hopping from the swing.

"What are we playing?" Lucy asked. "And I want to be on Jake's team."

"They don't have gloves," Pete said.

"That's true," Jake said. He walked over to Elizabeth. "Do they know how to play baseball?"

She shook her head. "Nope."

"How about we play a different game," Jake suggested.

Pete groaned. "Why?"

"Gianna and Lucy don't know how to play." Jake dropped an arm over his oldest son's shoulder and whispered loud enough for Elizabeth to hear, "To be honest, I don't think Elizabeth knows how to play either."

"What are we going to play instead?" Pete asked.

"How about hide-and-seek."

Pete, Ben, and Molly cheered while Lucy and Gianna just looked confused.

"Forty-four homes," Elizabeth said.

"I love that game," Gianna said. "Who is going to be it?"

"I'll be it," Jake said. He walked over to a huge tree in the middle of the yard, leaned his head against the trunk, and began to count slowly.

Pete and Ben took off running. Apparently they had a good place to hide.

Molly took each of the girls by the hand and ran across the lawn. She turned and looked at Elizabeth. "Aren't you coming? This is a great spot. I hide here all the time, and Dad never finds me."

"Sure."

The yard was large, and there were plenty of big trees they could hide behind. Molly ran past those without a second glance, so Elizabeth followed. Finally they came upon some buildings on the edge of a fenced pasture and crept inside one. It was dark and damp.

Lucy and Gianna giggled.

"Shh," Molly admonished quietly. "You don't want Daddy to hear us."

"Right," Gianna said in what Elizabeth imagined was supposed to be a whisper but fell far short.

Elizabeth inhaled and immediately wished she hadn't. She was a rodeo performer, so she was used to being around stock. It didn't smell like live animals in here, and she just hoped Molly hadn't led them to some animal cemetery.

"Ready or not, here I come!" Jake yelled, his voice carrying from the distance.

Lucy laughed and immediately covered her mouth with her hands. Molly opened the door a bit and then peered outside. She then turned back to look at them. "Daddy is going in the other direction. When I say *go*, run as fast as you can to the home base, okay?"

Gianna and Lucy nodded. Molly glanced over at Elizabeth, who nodded as well. After a minute, Molly turned and whispered, "Go."

The girls took off, sprinting as fast as their little legs could go. Elizabeth ran more slowly, intentionally lagging behind so that the girls would beat her.

Jake's back was to them, and he didn't turn around until they were nearly at the tree. When he spotted them, he ran in their direction, attempting to cut them off. As expected, the girls reached the tree in time to tag it. Elizabeth sped up as she tried to outrun Jake. Her fingers were tantalizingly close to home base when Jake's arms wrapped around her waist. In one smooth motion, he lifted her and spun her around.

"I got you," he said, triumph in his voice.

Elizabeth glanced up at him, a smile on her face. He looked back at her, a devilish grin on his. His eyes sparkled with mischief before they darkened with desire. Suddenly longing filled her, replacing every hint of playfulness.

"Oh, Mummy. You're out," Lucy said, mournfully.

"Sorry that you lost, Mummy," Gianna said. "But yay, Jake. You caught Mummy."

"I thought you would be able to run faster than that," Molly said. "Or I would have waited until Daddy was farther away."

"That's all right," Elizabeth said. "It's just a game, and games are supposed to be fun."

"I'm having fun," Gianna assured her.

"Me too," Lucy echoed. She looked at Jake. "Why are you still hugging Mummy?"

Molly glanced at them as if realizing for the first time that Elizabeth and her father were still entangled in each other's arms. Being in Jake's arms felt so natural that moving had never crossed Elizabeth's mind.

"I just wanted to be sure that she could stand on her own. She did run a long way," Jake said as he released her. "Remember, your mother isn't as young as you guys are."

"You'll pay for that," Elizabeth whispered.

"I look forward to it," he whispered back. Then he spoke louder. "Now I need to try to find Ben and Pete."

"You'll never find them," Molly said. "They have a good spot."

"Do you want me to help you find them, Jake?" Gianna asked, walking over and taking his hand. "I'm good at finding people. We play this game at home, and I win when I'm it."

"I would love your help," Jake said. He led Gianna to the tree house. "Let's look up there."

Slats had been nailed against the trunk, forming a ladder. Jake climbed the lowest three rungs and peered inside the tree house. He jumped down and looked at Gianna. "They aren't in there."

"Where can they be?" she asked.

At that moment, Pete and Ben came running from the other direction. They were laughing, and the sound reached Jake and Gianna.

"There they are, Jake," Gianna said, taking off running. "Come on so you can tag them."

Jake nodded and jogged toward his sons.

"Faster!" Gianna cried. "They're going to beat you."

Jake sped up, but it was too little too late. Pete and Ben touched home base seconds before Jake got there. Lucy and Molly joined Pete and Ben's celebration.

"It looks like Mummy is the only one you caught," Gianna said, giving his hand a sympathetic pat.

"That's okay. I don't mind," Jake said.

"That's good because you never win," Pete said.

"Are you losing on purpose?" Molly asked, suddenly suspicious.

"Are you winning on purpose?" Jake countered.

"Yes," she replied without taking a breath.

"Maybe you could try losing on purpose so I could win," Jake said.

She giggled and shook her head. "Nope."

The kids ran over to play on the swings, leaving Jake and Elizabeth alone. She leaned against the tree trunk and grinned at him. "Pretty sneaky. Turning the pressure back on her. Molly didn't notice you didn't answer her question."

"I've had years of practice. But I don't know how much longer that trick's going to work."

Elizabeth laughed as they walked across the lawn. She went inside and checked on the beef before joining Jake on the patio. "That was fun. Even though you caught me."

"It was." He gave her a long look. "Did you let me catch you?"

"Dinner won't be long."

He grinned. "Smooth. But not so smooth that I didn't notice you didn't answer my question."

"I guess you'll never know." She laughed and leaned back against her chair. "You know, you have a new fan in Gianna. She really likes you."

"What's not to like?"

"Good point. My daughter has excellent taste."

They laughed and talked quietly for a few more minutes before Elizabeth checked the time. "I need to call Molly in so she can help with the next steps."

"Thank you for letting her help you. It really means a lot to her."

"Of course. I enjoy her company. I'm just sorry that she pushed you aside that way."

"Are you apologizing for my daughter's behavior?" He laughed. "I don't see how you could possibly be responsible."

"I'm saying that I'm sorry if your feelings were hurt."

"They were a little bit. But I understand. Molly wanted to have some female bonding time with you. She didn't want me horning in on her fun."

Elizabeth grinned at him. "I wouldn't have minded you sticking around."

"It's better this way."

"How do you figure?"

"When I want to have some time alone with you, I'll remind her of today."

"When will that be?"

"As soon as we can manage."

She smiled as she contemplated spending more time in Jake's arms. Her lips tingled as she anticipated more hot kisses. If she could sneak one now, she would. But there were five sets of eyes who could look at them at any moment. She stood and waved to Molly. Then she grinned at him. "I'm free when you are."

"Now?" Molly asked, running over. Lucy and Gianna were behind her.

"Yes. We need to finish the meat pies and the Pavlova. The peas and potatoes will be easy."

"Easy-peasy," Gianna said, and then she and Lucy laughed at her play on words.

"Okay," Molly said. She looked at the twins. "I'll be back to play with you later."

"See you later," Gianna said, then she and Lucy ran off to play with the boys.

Elizabeth and Molly returned to the kitchen.

"Now we're about to do the best part," Elizabeth said as she took out the pastry sheets. "We could make our own puff pastry, but it's a lot of work and the store-bought ones are just as good."

She set the muffin tins on the counter, then showed Molly how to cut the pastry sheets to size. Molly was nervous as she did the first two, but once she had the hang of it, she relaxed and began to ask questions about Australia, which Elizabeth did her best to answer.

"When you guys go back, can I come and visit?"

"I would like that, but of course, we would need to ask your father."

"He could come too. Plus my brothers. It would be a lot of fun, and it wouldn't be fair if they had to stay home." Molly looked directly at Elizabeth. "You do like Pete and Ben too. Right?"

"I do. Your father and brothers would be welcome to come for a visit with you."

They placed the crust in the tins. Elizabeth removed the Pavlova and then set it on the dining room table where it would be out of the way for the time being. Then she put the pie crusts in the oven to brown.

"I think it is so cool that we'll each have our own pies. I might eat two."

"We're going to make twenty, so there will be enough for seconds. There should be some left over for tomorrow too. While they're cooking, let's peel the potatoes and boil the water."

"Dad makes mashed potatoes from the box."

Elizabeth squelched a frown. She wasn't a fan of those, but she understood the need to cut corners on occasion. There were only so many hours in the day and too many tasks for a single parent to complete. She just preferred to save time in other areas. Food was her love language, and she wanted people who ate at her table to savor every bite.

"Then he will love the ones we make for him," Elizabeth said, handing a vegetable peeler to Molly and keeping one for herself.

"Cooking is a lot of work," Molly said sometime later. They had peeled and cut the potatoes, filled the pie shells with meat, covered them, and set them back in the oven.

"It is. That's why I like to make enough food to have as leftovers the next day."

"That's smart. You know a lot of things that Daddy doesn't."

"Maybe. But your dad knows a lot of things that I don't know," Elizabeth said. "Plus he does a good job of taking care of you and your brothers."

"He won't let me get my ears pierced."

"Oh." That was a nice neutral response. Hopefully it would keep the conversation from veering into criticism. That thought was so ludicrous that Elizabeth could only shake her head. Of course Molly was going to complain about her father. She wouldn't have brought up the subject otherwise.

"He doesn't think I'm old enough."

"I see." Another noncommittal response. Like the first, it didn't end the conversation.

"Lucy and Gianna have pierced ears. How old were they when they got their ears pierced?"

"They were babies. But every family has their own rules. Just because I allow my girls to do something doesn't mean that your father is wrong to keep you from doing it. Do you know what I mean?"

"Sort of." Molly frowned. She understood, but that didn't mean she liked it.

"Good." Desperate to change the subject, Elizabeth redirected Molly back to their cooking project. But after they'd mashed the potatoes Molly picked up the conversation about earrings. "Since you know it's okay for kids younger than me to have their ears pierced, you should tell Daddy. Maybe he doesn't understand. You know, he's thinking about it like a dad, which is the wrong way. He should think about it like a mom would."

"Have you asked him?"

"Yes. He just said no. I think he thinks I'm too little."

Molly spoke slowly. Thoughtfully. "I'll go with you when you tell him that I'm old enough. We can show him Gianna's and Lucy's ears too."

"I think it would be better if you ask him. He might not like me butting into a family matter."

"Daddy likes you. He won't listen to me because I'm a kid."

Elizabeth blew out a breath. There didn't seem to be a way out of this. Not without hurting Molly's feelings. "Okay. We can ask him after dinner."

Hopefully Jake wouldn't get upset and toss her out on her ear.

Chapter Twelve

"**D**inner is ready," Molly announced proudly as she stepped onto the patio, a wide smile on her face. "Wait until you taste what we made."

"I know it's going to be extra good because you and Mummy made it together," Gianna said, beaming at her.

Molly nodded. "Thank you."

"I can hardly wait," Lucy said. "I'm starving."

They had eaten sandwiches and fruit for a late lunch, but that had been a while ago. The kids rushed over to the door. Molly held her arms out, blocking their entrance.

"You're in the way," Pete said. "How can we eat if we can't get in the house?"

She didn't budge. "Here are the rules. Number one. Walk very quietly. No stomping or running. Number two. No loud talking. We don't want the Pavlova to fall."

"The what?" Pete asked.

"The dessert," Elizabeth said. "And don't worry, Molly. It has set, so it will be fine."

"Well, they should be careful just in case."

"We'll be very quiet. Won't we?" Jake asked, making eye contact with each kid. He held Pete's gaze just a bit longer. The children nodded in agreement. "Good. Open the door, Molly."

Molly opened the screen door and then stepped aside. She gave each of her brothers a meaningful look as they passed her. Gianna and Lucy tiptoed in an exaggerated fashion as they went into the house.

Once everyone had washed their hands, they took their places at the dining room table.

"The table looks very nice," Jake said.

"Molly set it," Elizabeth said quickly. She smiled at Molly, who grinned proudly. "Since she worked so hard to cook this delicious meal, it's only right that the table look nice."

"I love meat pies," Lucy said. "My stomach can't wait to eat one."

After a quick blessing, Elizabeth began serving the meal, placing a meat pie on each plate. Jake followed, adding mashed potatoes and peas.

Molly held her breath while her father and brothers took a bite of their pies.

"This is really good," Pete said. "I never heard of a meat pie before, but I like it."

"Me too," Ben said.

Molly beamed and then took a bite. "I like it too. When we go to Australia, I'm going to eat them all the time."

"When are we going to Australia?" Pete asked.

"I want to come too," Ben added, looking around. "Am I going?"

"Hold on a minute," Jake said, looking from Elizabeth to Molly and back again. "Who said anything about going to Australia?"

Elizabeth felt Jake's eyes on her. She needed to straighten things out before the conversation got out of hand. "Molly and I were talking about Australia. I told her that all of you are welcome to visit anytime."

"So, you've made up your mind." Jake's voice held a hint of disappointment.

She should have known he would jump to that conclusion. "Not at all. Molly and I were just having a general conversation."

The smile he flashed her made her heart skip a beat. It felt good to know he wanted more time with her. Especially since she felt the same way about him.

"I see." He nodded. "It is a good idea. One that we should consider. Especially if the food is this good."

After that, Jake's kids spent the rest of the meal asking Lucy and Gianna what it was like to live in Australia.

When it was time for dessert, Molly stood. "Wait until you taste the Pavlova."

"Oh, we love Pavlova," Gianna said, rubbing her tummy.

Elizabeth had stored the dessert in an airtight container in the kitchen before Molly set the dining room table after it was done. Now she removed it and placed it on a tray. After putting fruit on top, she handed the tray to Molly, who carried it into the dining room. There was much oohing and aahing when she set the dessert on the table.

"You made that?" Pete asked, both skeptical and impressed.

Molly nodded. "Elizabeth helped."

Elizabeth and Jake exchanged amused smiles at the way Molly had framed her answer.

"Since you made it, you should get the first piece," Elizabeth said as she sliced the dessert.

"Can I have the second?" Ben asked.

"Sure," she said. "And don't worry. There's plenty."

Once everyone had a piece they began to eat. Unlike with the meat pies, Molly didn't wait for others to taste their food before taking a bite. Others soon followed suit.

Nobody spoke for a moment. Then the silence was replaced with groans of pleasure.

"You are the best cook, Molly," Ben said. "This is the best Pavlova I've ever had."

"It's the only Pavlova you've ever had," Pete pointed out. "But it is really good, Molly."

The compliments continued in between bites. When the last bit of dessert was gone, everyone leaned back in their chairs with satisfied smiles. Molly's smile had grown broader as the compliments had gotten more effusive. Now she was practically glowing.

"Since Elizabeth and Molly cooked, the rest of us will do the dishes," Jake said.

"Okay," Gianna said. "We know how to wash dishes."

"Yeah. We're big girls, so we help Mummy all the time," Lucy added.

Elizabeth watched with pride as her daughters hopped up, set their utensils on their plates, and walked carefully to the kitchen. After a moment, Pete and Ben did the same.

Molly reached for her dishes, but Jake stopped her. She glanced at him, a quizzical expression on her face.

He grinned. "You cooked, remember?"

"So, what do I do now?"

"Relax." Jake stacked Molly and Elizabeth's plates on his.

"Let's go sit on the patio," Elizabeth said.

"Okay." Molly looked at Jake. "When you're finished in here, Elizabeth wants to talk to you."

"About?"

"About getting my ears pierced like Lucy and Gianna."

"That's not exactly how we were going to talk about it," Elizabeth said, looking at Jake and trying to gauge his mood.

He shook his head and set the dishes back onto the table.

"Don't say no, Daddy. Please." Molly clasped her hands as if in prayer.

He pulled out the chair beside her, sat, and took her hands into his. "I wasn't going to say no. If you want to get your ears pierced, I guess it's okay."

"Really?" she asked, hope dripping from her voice.

"Really."

Molly shrieked and then jumped up, throwing her arms around Jake's neck. "Thank you. Thank you. Thank you."

The other kids came running to see what the commotion was about.

"What's going on?" Pete asked.

"Daddy said I can get my ears pierced."

"Is that all? I thought it was something important," Pete said, shaking his head.

"It *is* important," Molly said, looking annoyed at her brother.

"You can wear earrings like me and Lucy," Gianna said.

"I don't know what kind I want," Molly said. "There are so many pretty earrings to choose from."

"When are you going to get them pierced?" Gianna asked.

"I don't know." Molly looked at Elizabeth. "Will you go with me and Daddy?"

Elizabeth looked over at Jake before answering. He nodded his approval. "Yes. When do you want to go?"

"Can we go tomorrow?"

"Yes. If it's okay with your dad."

"It is," Jake said.

Molly smiled and hugged her waist. "This is so exciting."

The younger kids grabbed the glasses and napkins and carried them into the kitchen. Too excited to sit still, Molly followed them.

"I hope you know that I didn't bring up getting her ears pierced. That was all Molly," Elizabeth said.

"I do. Molly has talked about it for a while. To be honest, I didn't have a good reason to say no. I was trying to keep her from growing up too fast. She already acts like a little mother around here. But since Gianna and Lucy have pierced ears, I guess it's fine."

"We'll get her some nice, age-appropriate earrings."

"I know you will." He smiled and appeared to be about to say something. Instead he rapped his knuckles on the table. Elizabeth would rather he say what was on his mind as opposed to keeping it to himself.

"What is it?"

One corner of his mouth lifted in a sexy grin. "I should have known you could tell that I had something on my mind."

"I do. So just tell me, and we'll deal with the fallout."

"There shouldn't be any fallout. This is something good." He smiled. "Our kids get along great with each other. And my kids adore you. Not to be vain, but your girls like me too. And I know that you really, *really* like me."

Elizabeth punched his shoulder. "Oh, you do, do you?"

"Yes. And I really, *really* like you too. So let's spend more time together. Not just the occasional dates when we can get babysitters. I would like to see you more, even if that means all seven of us and not just the two of us. It's not fair to ask you to drive out here all the time, so I'm willing to pack up the kids and come to the cabin."

Elizabeth shook her head.

"You don't want to see me more?"

She laughed. "No. Yes."

"Which one?"

She inhaled and then blew out the breath. "Yes, I want to see you. No, it's not necessary for you to bring the kids to the cabin. I don't mind driving. Besides, there's so much more room here. We can improvise at the cabin every now and then, but I do prefer to eat together. Besides, my girls love playing in the tree house and on the swings."

"If you're sure."

"I am."

After Jake and the younger kids finished cleaning the kitchen, everyone went back outside to enjoy the evening.

Pete and Molly were trying to teach the younger kids how to walk on their hands. Every time one of them landed on the ground, Elizabeth winced. The kids only laughed and tried again.

"Don't worry. Kids bounce," Jake said.

"I hope nobody's dinner comes back up," she said.

"We finished eating forty minutes ago, so that won't be a problem."

"Has that much time passed? I really should get the girls and get going."

"What's the rush? The kids are having a great time. I don't have to tell you how much I'm enjoying your company."

"In that case…" Elizabeth leaned back in her chair, letting the cool breeze blow over her body. She closed her eyes and a peace settled over her. She could get used to this.

"Owww!" The screech followed by crying filled the air, and Elizabeth's eyes flew open. Jake was already on his feet, and she jumped up and raced behind him. They reached the kids in seconds.

"Sorry, Ben," Gianna said. "I didn't mean it. It was an accident."

"What happened?" Jake asked. His voice sounded shaky and louder than usual.

"Me and Ben crashed," Gianna said. "And my feet hit his face."

Jake lifted his son's chin and studied his face carefully. His hand trembled. "No blood. Shake it off, bud. You're a tough rancher."

Ben turned and took two steps away. He squared his shoulders as if trying to stop crying.

"What? He's not a tough rancher. He's a little boy." Elizabeth said sharply. She walked over to Ben, stooped down and held out her arms. Still sniffling, he went into her embrace and leaned his head against her breast. She kissed his forehead and rubbed his back. "It'll be okay."

Ben sighed and snuggled closer.

"Does Ben need a doctor?" Gianna asked in a quivering voice. Her eyes filled with tears.

"No," Elizabeth said quickly. "I can take care of him."

"I didn't do it on purpose," Gianna repeated, wiping a tear from her face.

Lucy took her sister's hand and patted it. "It's okay, Gianna."

"I know you didn't mean to hurt him," Elizabeth said. "And Ben knows that too."

He looked over at Gianna and echoed Elizabeth's words.

Elizabeth looked at her girls. "Why don't you two go and swing for a while."

"Okay, Mummy," Lucy said, leading her sister away. Gianna glanced over her shoulder, and Elizabeth gave her an encouraging nod.

"How about some ice for your face?" Elizabeth asked Ben. He stared up at her and nodded against her breast. She looked at Molly and Pete who hadn't moved. Clearly they were concerned about their brother. "We'll be right back."

Elizabeth stood, wrapped her arm around Ben's thin

shoulder, and steered him toward the house. When they reached the kitchen, she grabbed a dish towel and filled it with ice. "This is going to be cold, but it's going to help. Okay?"

Ben sniffed and nodded. Elizabeth pressed the towel against his red cheek. The color was starting to fade, but he might have a little bruise in a couple of days.

"Hold that against your face, okay, sweetie?" she asked.

"Okay. Can I go back outside?"

"Of course."

He slipped his hand into hers and gave her a wide smile. When they stepped onto the patio, he leaned against her side. "Can I sit on your lap for a minute? You know, to help me feel better."

"If you think it would help," she said.

He nodded. Elizabeth didn't think he was still in pain, but she knew a little bit of affection went a long way. She sat down. Holding the ice pack in his hand, Ben scooted onto her lap and leaned against her. Elizabeth smiled to herself and wrapped her arms around him. She sang softly to him, and he smiled at her. A feeling of contentment filled her as she rocked the little boy in her arms.

Molly looked at her brother in Elizabeth's arms, her eyes narrowed and her lips pinched. Then she looked up at Jake. "I know how to take care of Ben."

"Yes, you do. But he wanted Elizabeth." Jake managed to keep the hurt out of his voice. He'd felt the sting of rejection as his son bypassed him in favor of Elizabeth. *He* was Ben's parent, not Elizabeth. But then, he hadn't offered Ben comfort and Elizabeth had. Not wanting to baby his son, he'd offered strength. In retrospect, that had been the wrong approach.

Afraid his child had been seriously hurt, he'd forgotten to ask *WWMD?* He'd simply reacted.

"Why?"

"He likes her." That was the best answer he could come up with. When Molly's frown only deepened, he knew he had a problem on his hands and that he had to do his best to solve it before it grew. "But that doesn't mean he doesn't need you."

Molly looked at him. This time her expression was not as easy to read, leaving him at a loss for words. No doubt she was dealing with the same mixed emotions that he was. She'd loved spending time with Elizabeth and had even shoved Jake aside so the two of them could be alone. She hadn't seemed bothered by the fact that her brothers liked Elizabeth too. But that was before Ben had turned to her. Did Molly look at Elizabeth as a threat now as he had for a few rough moments? Maybe. But Jake was an adult and could recognize when he was being ridiculous. As much as she liked to think of herself as a mini adult, Molly was only a child and didn't possess that ability.

Jake held out his hand. She looked at it for a minute before she took it. "Let's go for a walk."

"Where?"

"Nowhere in particular. I just didn't get a chance to spend much time with you today. You were with Elizabeth."

"We were cooking," she pointed out.

"And you did a great job. But a little Dad-and-Molly time would be good too."

She heaved out a breath. "If you say so."

They walked in silence for a couple of minutes. He searched for something to say to make the situation better. "Tell me about the earrings you want to get. You said something about flowers and butterflies."

"Yes. They come in a lot of colors. How many can I get? Can I get a jewelry box like Gianna's and Lucy's? They brought them from Australia. Do you think they sell that kind in Montana?"

He shrugged. He had no idea since he'd never seen them. "I don't know. But if not, I'm sure we can find a nice jewelry box for you."

That seemed to satisfy her.

"I'm better now," Ben called. Molly and Jake turned as he ran over to them.

"Let me see your face," Molly said.

Ben turned to the right and to the left. "Elizabeth put ice on it. And she let me sit on her lap. She sang me a song and told me a story. Now I can play again. Here she comes."

Jake turned as Elizabeth approached. She was smiling, and he breathed a sigh of relief. He was glad that her annoyance had passed. His had too.

"I'll go keep an eye on Ben so he doesn't get hurt again," Molly said and then walked away, making a big point to ignore Elizabeth. Clearly Jake hadn't gotten through after all.

"Okay," Jake said. Elizabeth didn't seem to notice Molly's attitude, and he didn't point it out.

"So much for our quiet moment," Elizabeth said, coming to stand beside him. She bumped his shoulder with hers. The twins ran over to Ben. Gianna said something Jake couldn't hear, and then Ben and Gianna hugged.

"I hope you didn't mind taking care of Ben."

"Of course not." She gave him a perceptive look. "I hope *you* didn't mind. It's clear Molly did."

Elizabeth had picked up on the attitude after all. "She's used to taking care of him."

"And you? Did I step on your toes?"

He blew out a long breath. "To be honest, I was a bit jealous there for a minute."

"Why?"

"I guess because I've had Ben to myself for six years. I've been both father and mother to him. Having him reject me was a bit of a shock to my system." He gave a self-conscious smile. "I'm embarrassed to admit all of that."

"Don't be silly."

"That's what I told myself."

"That's not what I meant. I mean it's silly to be embarrassed by how you feel. We all have negative emotions. I probably would feel the same way if my girls preferred someone else to me." She took his hand and gazed into his eyes. Hers were filled with compassion and understanding. "We need to be honest about how we feel. Even if it's an emotion we aren't proud of. And we're going to have to understand how the other feels."

"You're something else, you know that?"

"I hope you mean that in a good way."

"Only the best way."

She smiled at him, and his heart thudded in his chest. He appreciated her kindness, but he would be lying if he denied the impact her body had on him. They were close enough for him to inhale her sweet scent with every breath. He wondered if he could sneak a kiss without one of the kids seeing.

The more he was around her, the more he wanted to be with her.

Ben and the twins ran over then. Ben grabbed Elizabeth's hand and smiled at her. "What are we going to do now?"

"It's time for me and the twins to go home."

"I wish we could stay here all the time," Lucy said.

"Not me," Gianna said. "I miss home. And I want to see Grandma and Grandpa."

Lucy thought for a moment. "Yes, me too. But I wish we could come here all the time on vacation."

Jake glanced over at Elizabeth. Hearing her daughters talk about missing home and their grandparents had to be tugging on her heartstrings. Every time he thought that she might be leaning toward staying in Montana, something happened to pull her back toward Australia. He understood how difficult her decision must be. He also knew it would be wrong to try to convince her to stay. She was already being pulled in different directions. He didn't want to add to her pressure.

That didn't mean he would stand idly by and hope for the best. He'd never been the type to let luck or fate rule his life. He would show Elizabeth how he felt. Hopefully that would be enough to keep her here.

Chapter Thirteen

Elizabeth looked around the main dining room of the Library, a restaurant in Bronco Valley, and sighed. It seemed as if everyone in town was attending the bridal shower for Winona Cobbs, one of the most popular people in Bronco. Elizabeth smiled as she thought about the ninetysomething-year-old woman who was about to take the plunge. Talk about a leap of faith.

"Isn't this just the best?" Amy said to Elizabeth. She spread her arm out, encompassing everything from the pink-and-white balloons forming high arches to the enormous bouquets of flowers perfuming the air to the trays overflowing with every hors d'oeuvre known to man. That gesture also took in the fountains of pink drinks and the five-piece band playing songs from the fifties. Clearly no expense had been spared. Given the bride's advanced age, Elizabeth would expect no less.

Although Elizabeth was a relative newcomer to town, she'd been invited along with her sisters. She recognized some of the guests and had been introduced to the others. Naturally Winona's daughter, Daisy, was in attendance as well as her granddaughter, Wanda. They were talking to Winona's great-grandchildren, Evan and Vanessa.

"It definitely is the biggest bridal shower I have ever

attended," Elizabeth replied. She and her sisters were sitting together at one of the numerous tables. They'd played some of the traditional bridal shower games as well as a few Elizabeth had never heard of.

"That's because everyone is so happy that Winona and Stanley have finally gotten past their jealousy and quarreling. Now they're finally getting together for good, and everyone wants to be a part of it," Tori said.

Elizabeth didn't know much of the backstory, but to her way of thinking, it wasn't important. The past didn't count. What mattered was these two people were getting their happy ending.

Winona had been circulating and came upon them in time to hear Tori's comment. She looked at Elizabeth and her sisters and tossed her long purple print scarf over her shoulder before replying, "I can't tell you how much I regret making Stanley wait so long before agreeing to marry him and setting a date. Looking back, there was too much quarreling. I should have done more to assure him that he had nothing to be jealous about. He is my one and only."

Winona met each of their eyes before continuing. "In my defense, I still had the scars from my relationship with Josiah all those years ago. I know we were more or less just teenagers ourselves, but even so…" She sighed. The man she was referring to was her former love—and the father of her child—rancher Josiah Abernathy. They had fallen for each other decades ago, but when he'd gotten Winona pregnant, it had been a scandal that had rocked their ranching community. "I loved him and I felt betrayed when he lied and told me our baby had been stillborn. But now, I've found my daughter again, and all of that is behind me. My scars are healed, and I'm ready to start the next chapter of my life."

"I'm sure he's just happy to finally make everything official," Elizabeth said.

Winona nodded and then looked at her intently. After studying her a moment, she took Elizabeth's hand. "The past is present. The present will pass."

Elizabeth didn't know what the older woman meant. Before she could ask for clarification, Daisy came over and whisked Winona away.

"What was that about?" Elizabeth asked her sisters.

"She claims to have second sight," Amy said, "so maybe she was doing some type of fortune telling. And to be fair, she has given similar fortunes to other couples in Bronco."

"Really?"

Faith shrugged. "Winona is a bit odd, but she means well. And she's completely harmless."

"Okay," Elizabeth said. She had her own quirks, so who was she to judge?

The sisters rose and began mingling, talking with other partygoers. Although Elizabeth didn't know all of them, it didn't take her long to notice that a certain theme ran through every conversation. No matter the topic, they inevitably got around to talking about Jake.

"When is the big date?" a smiling woman asked. She'd been part of a larger group Elizabeth had met earlier, and she struggled to recall the other woman's name.

"What big date?" Elizabeth answered. After trying out a few names—Candy? Mandy? Brandy?—she gave up and decided to just talk.

"You know. You and Jake McCreery. Everyone has seen you around town together. It's common knowledge that you and your girls have been spending time with him and his kids at the ranch. Marriage is the next logical step."

"Jake and I have not discussed marriage once," Elizabeth said emphatically.

"Have you guys touched the pearl necklace yet? That will definitely speed things up a bit."

"What pearl necklace?" Elizabeth asked, then immediately regretted it. She didn't want to prolong this conversation. "Never mind. I'm not interested in speeding up anything. I like things just the way they are."

"I'll tell you, just in case you change your mind. The necklace has magical powers. At least when it comes to matters of the heart. It helps get couples together. It could work with you and Jake," the woman said. She winked and then walked away.

"What are you frowning about?" Faith asked, coming over to Elizabeth and handing her a plate with meatballs on it. They returned to their table and sat down.

Elizabeth exhaled and forced a smile. She didn't want to be a Negative Nelly at such a happy event. She recounted the conversation between bites of the tasty hors d'oeuvres.

"You and Jake have been spending a lot of time together. Naturally that will stir up talk. I'm sure Randi isn't the only person thinking you're about to take a trip down the aisle."

"Why?"

"Because Bronco is a small town. There's not much else to do here," Tori joked.

"I'll have to deduct a point for that."

"What does that mean?" Amy asked.

"Inside joke that Jake and I share."

"Inside joke. Hmm," Tori said.

"You seem really happy with Jake," Faith said. "Are you? Can you see yourself making it work with him?"

Elizabeth fantasized for a moment about being married to Jake. Spending their days and nights together would be wonderful. Then reality hit. "Can you imagine being the mother of five children? It is hard enough with just two. It's not as if any of them are teens and for the most part self-sufficient."

"At least none of them are in diapers," Faith said.

"There is that, I suppose," Elizabeth said with a laugh before she sobered. "I've lived my life on the road. So have my girls. Jake and his kids are rooted to the ranch. I can't ask them to suddenly change their lives and travel the rodeo circuit in Australia any more than I can ask Gianna and Lucy to live on a ranch in America."

"I thought you wanted to settle down when the girls start school."

"I do. Now that Arlo is gone, roots are more important than ever. That feeling of having a home. A place where you belong," she glanced at her sisters. "But school isn't compulsory in Australia until they're six."

"Does that mean you're going back?"

Elizabeth pushed her empty dish into the middle of the table and then rubbed her forehead. "I don't know. That's where our roots are. The place that has always been their home. Arlo's family is there. They can help the girls remember him. But you are all here. And the girls are making friends now. We're all happy here." She sighed. "I thought I had time to plan my next move, but time is slipping away and I haven't decided anything. I have to do something. I can't remain in limbo forever."

"Don't think you have to make a decision soon based on needing to vacate the cabin," Tori said. "You're welcome to stay there as long as you need."

"Thanks. I don't want to inconvenience you."

"You aren't."

"Well, you can worry about that later," Amy said, putting her arm through Elizabeth's. "This is a party. Let's have fun."

"That sounds like a plan I can get behind," she said, shoving away her troubling thoughts. A celebration of love was no place for worrying about her problems.

After a night of troubled sleep, Elizabeth woke up early the next morning. She took a quick shower and then dressed in shorts and a favorite T-shirt. She and the girls were going to spend a quiet day here in the cabin. That was good since she wasn't in the frame of mind to interact with other people. She needed time to hunker down with her little family.

She was setting breakfast on the table when Gianna and Lucy barreled into the kitchen. They were wearing sundresses she'd bought for them at the mall in Wonderstone Ridge when they'd gotten Molly's ears pierced. The three girls had each gotten four matching dresses.

"Don't you both look pretty," Elizabeth said.

"Thank you," Gianna said.

"Is today a special day?"

Arlo had liked to create their very own holidays. They'd celebrate by eating treats and creating special banners. He also invented games that the girls always won. Although her heart had not always been in it, Elizabeth had kept the tradition alive. Now the girls created their own random holidays.

"Nope," Lucy said. "We just like these dresses."

"Daddy said we look like princesses," Gianna said. "Didn't he, Lucy?"

Elizabeth's heart stuttered. She knew the girls didn't have specific memories of Arlo. They'd been so young when he'd died. Elizabeth often told them stories about him and reminded them of how much he'd loved them. How proud of them he'd been. Had they decided to make up a story of their own? Creating a memory of their father telling them how pretty they looked in dresses he had never seen them wearing?

"Did he?" Elizabeth asked, going along with them. She knew her little girls missed their daddy and wished he was around.

Lucy nodded. "But he said they were too pretty to wear on the swings."

Goose bumps rose on Elizabeth's arms. "When did he say that?"

"When we bought them," Gianna said, digging her spoon into her cereal.

"You were right there when he said it," Lucy pointed out. "Don't you remember?"

Elizabeth's heart hammered and she felt her mouth go dry. "*Jake* said that."

The girls nodded. "Yes."

"Jake is not your daddy."

"We know. But Ben said that it was okay if we pretend that he's our daddy. And we said he could pretend you're his mummy."

"When did this all happen?" Elizabeth tried to sound calm, but panic leaked into her voice.

Lucy shrugged. Time was a developing concept for them. Not to mention totally unimportant. "You did make him feel better after Gianna kicked him."

"I didn't mean to," Gianna was quick to point out. "It was an accident."

"I know. But it happened," Lucy said and then grinned at her sister. "But he still loves you."

"And I love him," Gianna said. "You must love him too, Mummy. You let him sit on your lap that time you fixed his face."

"You even sang the feel better song to him. You only sing that to me and Gianna," Lucy said. "So it must be okay for him to say you're his mummy."

Elizabeth marveled at their logic. It was all so simple to them.

"Ben's mum died and our daddy died. He needs a mum and we need a daddy," Gianna explained. "So we're going to share."

"Is that right?" Elizabeth managed to say.

Gianna looked directly at her. "You always say it's nice to share."

There was nothing she could say to that, so she only nodded.

The girls nodded and then resumed eating. When they talked, it was about their favorite pictures in their new coloring books. Clearly choosing a new father and volunteering her services as mother to Ben was not a big deal to them. But for her it was gigantic. Not because she didn't like Ben. He was a sweetie and had carved a place in her heart.

Things were spinning out of control. First the gossips in town were having a field day talking about her and Jake. Now this. It was one thing when hers was the only heart at risk. And Jake's. But now their children were part of the equation. They were all becoming attached to each other. Worse, they were claiming her and Jake as parents. If things didn't work out, their children would be hurt. They'd lost parents once. They didn't need to experience that pain a second time.

She needed to talk to Jake. They needed to get a handle on the situation while there was still time. Getting their families together had seemed like a good idea at the time. The kids all got along well, and everyone was happy. Of course, everyone was happy when things went well. They would be in a world of hurt if things went bad. Even if there wasn't a bad breakup, they would all be heartbroken if she and the girls returned to Australia. But that wasn't reason enough to stay in Bronco.

The thought of denying Gianna and Lucy half of their heritage and keeping them apart from half of their family— the part that could tell them about their dad—nagged at her. Staying in Montana would be like erasing Arlo from their lives. Excluding his way of life from their future would be a horrible thing to do to them.

She liked Jake. No—her feelings went much deeper than that. She was falling in love with him. At another time that knowledge would fill her with joy. Now it only distressed her. Because she had to put on the brakes until she knew the right thing to do for all of them.

Jake ended the phone call and smiled. Elizabeth was bringing the girls over. It was an unexpected surprise, since they'd planned to spend the day apart. She'd told him that she'd fallen way behind on housework and needed to catch up. He also had piles of dirty clothes begging for his attention. Even so, when she'd said she wanted to come over, he instantly changed his plans. The laundry could wait.

The past few weeks had been clarifying. He realized that he'd met the woman he wanted to spend the rest of his life with. After losing Maggie, he didn't think he would ever find love again, so he hadn't even bothered to look. Love had found him anyway. He was in love with Elizabeth. He hoped—believed—she felt the same. They would find a way to make a relationship work—here in Bronco or in Australia.

It would take work to blend their families. Five kids living under one roof meant five different personalities finding a way to get along. Sure, it was working now, but it wouldn't be long before Molly was a teenager. Then Pete. Those years would bring their own challenges. Even so, Jake was up for it because he knew the good would always outweigh the bad.

When Elizabeth and the girls arrived, his kids ran out to greet them before they had even gotten out of the car. Then, as expected, they all ran into the backyard to play.

"Hi," he said to Elizabeth once they were alone. He pulled her into his arms and kissed her deeply. They'd agreed that they wouldn't expose the kids to any public displays of affection because it might be confusing for them. But the kids weren't around to see. Besides, he believed it was time to let the kids know they could become a family. Hopefully Elizabeth would agree.

"Hi," she said, pulling away and ending the kiss much sooner than he would have liked.

He looked into her face. She wasn't smiling, and his stomach plunged to his toes. "What's wrong?"

"We need to talk."

Like everyone in a relationship, he hated the sound of those words. "I can see that something is bothering you. Whatever it is, we can work through it together."

She shook her head. "*Together* is the problem. I think we're getting ahead of ourselves, Jake. We need to take a step back."

"What do you mean 'take a step back'?" Clearly he was alone in his belief that they were on their way to becoming a family.

She looked somewhere over his shoulder. "We've been spending a lot of time together. Too much time together. The kids are getting attached. We need to be sure of our feelings and what we want before we move to the next level."

Jake could only stare at her. Elizabeth was saying *we*, but he had a feeling she was talking about herself. *She* wasn't sure if her feelings were real. *She* was having doubts about the future. *She* wanted to step back from him.

He considered trying to convince her that his feelings were real and that they belonged together, but he wouldn't. You couldn't talk a person into loving you. Either they loved you or they didn't.

Maybe she wasn't over her husband yet. It wasn't out of the question. Arlo had only been gone two years. It had taken him three times that long to get over Maggie and open his heart again. It would be wrong not to give Elizabeth the time she needed.

He loved Elizabeth and would do whatever it took to make her happy. If that meant stepping back and giving her space, then he would. That was the noble thing to do. The right thing. He just hoped it wouldn't take her six years to get over her grief.

"So what do you want to do?" Somehow he kept his voice calm.

"Take a break." Her voice was soft, but he heard the pain and conflict there.

He'd expected her to say those words, but hearing them was still a dagger to his heart. "If that's what you need, I'll do it."

She nodded, clearly relieved that he hadn't argued. "Okay. I'll get the girls, and then we'll be gone."

"What should I tell Molly? Do you want her to stop being your helper?"

Regret crossed her face. "I think we can take a week or so off. I'll still pay her, of course."

"That's not necessary. I'll just explain that we decided to take a break. She'll understand."

"I hope so." She sounded so sad, he wondered why she was doing this. Taking a break obviously wasn't making her happy.

They stood there for a few seconds, looking at each other. It was as if neither of them wanted to face the reality that this was goodbye. The sorrow was coming off Elizabeth in waves. Then, as if she realized there was nothing more to say, she turned and walked into the backyard to gather her girls. Molly, Pete, and Ben returned with them.

"Let's go, girls," Elizabeth said, opening the back passenger door.

Gianna and Lucy looked at the car and then ran over to Jake. They each give him a tight hug. He held them tight before releasing them. They might not have been children of his body, but they were daughters in his heart.

"Bye, Jake," they said. Then they turned and ran back to the car. They waved one last time before they hopped into the vehicle.

He stood there, unable to move, watching as the three of them drove out of his life.

Chapter Fourteen

"Why did they leave so fast?" Pete asked, looking down the driveway as Elizabeth's car disappeared from view.

"Yeah, they just got here," Ben said, kicking a rock.

Jake looked at his children. He waited for Molly to chime in, but she didn't say a word. She only tugged on her T-shirt.

"Elizabeth and I decided not to see each other for a while," he told his children.

"Does that mean Gianna and Lucy won't come over?" Ben asked. "And that we can't go over to their house either?"

"Yes."

"Aww. I like them a lot," Ben said sadly.

"I know," Jake said softly.

"When will they be coming back?"

"I don't know," he said honestly. He was just as sad as his son, but he needed to be strong for them.

"I'm going to miss them," Ben said.

"Me too," Pete added. His voice was low, and Jake had to strain to hear it. "I like having them around. Lucy and Gianna are like little sisters. And Elizabeth felt like a mom."

"I know you said we're better on our own, but I like when Elizabeth is here," Ben said. "She makes me happy. So do Gianna and Lucy."

Jake brushed his hand over his youngest son's hair. "It is

better having them around. I hope they'll come back soon. But in the meantime, we'll be all right."

"It doesn't feel all right," Ben said, wiping a tear from his face. "It feels really bad."

Jake pulled his sons into his arms, doing his best to comfort them. After a minute, the boys pulled away. They trudged to the backyard, but no laughter followed them. Only silence.

"It's my fault," Molly said once her brothers were gone.

"What is?"

"Elizabeth leaving us."

"This isn't your fault."

"I was mean to her. I like her, but I was jealous that Ben liked her better. I should have been nicer. I didn't even say bye to her that day."

"That was a long time ago. Elizabeth knows that you like her. And she likes you too."

"Then why is she leaving us?"

"This is something between Elizabeth and me. Believe me, it has nothing to do with you."

Molly's brow wrinkled in thought. "I still need to apologize for being mean to her."

"Okay. And you'll see that she never held that against you."

"I'll apologize at the Bronco Spring Sing."

The Bronco Spring Sing was the brainchild of the high school chorale teacher. The Bronco Summer Family Rodeo had been a huge success in recent years, and so she thought it would be a good idea to showcase other talented Bronco residents, especially students of all ages. The Spring Sing was scheduled for this Saturday afternoon. He and Elizabeth had planned to take the kids together. But that was before they'd decided to take a break. "We don't know that she'll be there."

"But she has to come," Molly cried. "We're singing a song together."

"Who is?"

"All of us. Me and Pete and Ben and Gianna and Lucy. We've been practicing for a long time. You have to let us go."

"Of course I'll take you and your brothers. But I can't promise that Gianna and Lucy will be there."

"Can you ask her? Please?"

Jake shook his head. Molly's pleading just about broke his heart, but he'd just promised Elizabeth that he would give her the space that she needed. He couldn't turn around a few days later and tell her to bring Gianna and Lucy to the Spring Sing where they would see each other again. He would do his part and take his kids. Hopefully Gianna and Lucy would convince Elizabeth to bring them.

Then he would have the chance to see Elizabeth again, if only from a distance.

On the morning of the Bronco Spring Sing, the kids woke up early. After practically swallowing their breakfast whole, they ran upstairs where they stayed until it was time to leave. They hurried downstairs and ran to the SUV. Molly was wearing a pink floral sundress that she'd gotten when she'd had her ears pierced, and the boys were wearing blue striped dress shirts and khaki shorts.

They talked among themselves as Jake drove to town. They were getting out of the SUV when Elizabeth pulled into the parking spot next to him. The kids waited until Gianna and Lucy were out of the car before grabbing each other in a group hug.

"We want to sit together," Molly said, her glance encompassing Jake and Elizabeth.

"Yeah," Gianna added. "We missed everybody."

"My heart was sad before, but now it's happy again," Lucy said.

"Mine too," Ben added. He walked over to Elizabeth and gave her a big smile. "Aren't you happy to see me again?"

She nodded. "Yes. I'm happy to see all of you."

Ben took that as his invitation to hug Elizabeth, and he wrapped his arms around her waist. Her arms went around him, and she brushed a kiss on his head. Pete nudged Ben aside so he could get a hug.

"I missed you, Jake," Gianna said, coming over and embracing him.

"Me too," Lucy said, wrapping her arms around him.

Jake's heart swelled with emotion, and he swallowed hard before answering. When he spoke, his voice was rough. "I missed you both too."

Molly hung back for a second before she approached Elizabeth, who held out her arms. Then she rushed over. "I'm sorry I was mean to you that time, Elizabeth."

"I know," Elizabeth said. Still holding Molly in her arms, she leaned back and looked into her face. "Don't give it a second thought, okay?"

"So you forgive me?"

"I never held it against you. But yes, I forgive you."

Molly sighed and leaned against Elizabeth for a minute. Then she pulled away and looked at the other kids. "We need to go inside."

As one, the kids followed Molly.

When Jake and Elizabeth were alone, he gave her a serious look. "I hope you know I didn't set any of this up."

She nodded. "I know."

"You asked for space, and I intend to give it to you." No matter how it broke his heart.

"I appreciate that."

"You're looking good," Jake said. Whether she was wearing a simple blouse, skirt, and sandals like today or the red dress she'd worn on their first date, looking at her made his pulse race. He might've been giving her the space she needed, but that didn't require him to hide his attraction to her. He wanted her to remember their fun times, wanted her to remember how good their kisses had felt.

She smiled and brushed her hand over her white denim skirt, drawing his eyes to her slender body. "Thanks."

"Are you okay with sitting together?" he asked. "If not…"

"It's fine."

He opened the door to the convention center and gestured for her to go ahead of him. A sign in the entrance directed them to a midsize room, so they walked down the hall together.

She turned to him. "What is this Bronco Spring Sing?"

"I don't know any more than you," he said. "This is the first time it's been held. I've decided to just go with the flow."

"That's probably best. My girls were so determined to come today." She lifted her arms and let them drop to her sides. "So here I am."

The first two rows were filled, so they took seats in the third row. Elizabeth looked around. "Where are the kids?"

"I suppose they're backstage."

"Why would they be backstage?"

"You don't know?"

She shook her head, sending her hair flying over her shoulders. Suddenly he had an intense desire to pull her into his arms and bury his face in her hair. He fisted his hands so he wouldn't give in to that temptation. "Know what?"

"They're performing in the show."

"Really? What are they singing? When did they decide all this?"

"I don't know the answers to either of those questions. I just know they're going to be singing together."

The seats around Elizabeth and Jake quickly filled and before long nearly every chair in the room was occupied. The master of ceremony took the stage and welcomed everyone to the inaugural Bronco Spring Sing. She then introduced the pianist. The first performer was a girl of about twelve who sang a solo. When she finished, the crowd cheered. She grinned and bowed before skipping from the stage.

There were several more participants, each of whom sang with boundless enthusiasm and varying degrees of talent.

Finally, Jake's and Elizabeth's kids took the stage. Jake's chest puffed with pride before the kids even sang a word. The girls looked sweet in their matching dresses, and the boys managed to remain unruffled. Elizabeth glanced over at him. The bright smile on her face gave him hope. Surely she could see that they belonged together.

"What is the name of your group?" the emcee asked, placing the microphone in front of Gianna's face.

She took the microphone. "My name is Gianna Freeman."

She passed the microphone to her left, and the crowd chuckled.

"And I'm Lucy Freeman."

The emcee shook her head as each child took the mic, said their name, and then passed it along. Molly was last. After introducing herself, she handed the microphone back to the emcee who placed the microphone in a stand, adjusted the height, then stepped away. Molly organized the kids into a semicircle, then counted to four. After they had sung the first lines of the lyrics, Elizabeth gasped.

Confused, Jake turned to look at her. "Are you all right?"

She nodded. "They're singing 'Waltzing Matilda.' Arlo used to sing it to the girls every night. It was a Freeman tradition. His parents sang it to him when he was a boy. Now Lucy and Gianna taught it to your kids."

Jake covered her hand with his, listening as the kids sang the next verses. When they finished the tune, the kids joined hands and bowed. Jake jumped to his feet, whistling loudly through his fingers as the rest of the audience applauded. He might've been biased, but theirs was the best performance of the afternoon.

Once the last act finished their song, all of the participants returned to the stage and bowed together. Then they scattered in every which way.

Jake glanced at Elizabeth. She still seemed to be emotional and lost in her thoughts. "I'll round up the kids and bring them all back here."

She nodded. "Thank you."

Elizabeth watched as Jake crossed the room, weaving between clusters of children. Their kids had split into several groups and were goofing around with their friends. Gianna and Lucy, ordinarily glued to each other's side, were actually standing in separate groups. That little bit of progress gave her joy. Elizabeth wanted her girls to be close yet independent.

Elizabeth's eyes traveled around the room until she located Ben, Pete, and Molly. Over the past weeks they had made their own places in her heart. She'd missed them terribly these past few days. She'd grown used to Pete's jokes, Ben's affectionate hugs, and Molly's curiosity. There was no way she could walk away from them.

Gianna went over, grabbed Jake's hand, and smiled up at him. He said something to her that made her laugh.

Elizabeth had missed Jake so much. She'd missed how contented she felt around him, missed how much he made her laugh. She'd been tempted to call him so many times this past week, just to hear his voice, but stubbornly she hadn't.

But she wasn't the only one who'd missed him. Gianna and Lucy had missed him too. Several times a day they'd asked when they could go back to the ranch. They'd wanted to play with Molly, Pete, and Ben. Wanted Jake to give them pony rides. Her daughters loved the McCreerys. In their minds, they were a family. It didn't matter to them that they didn't share a drop of blood. Given the fact that most of the Hawkinses didn't share genes, Elizabeth knew biology wasn't the most important thing. Love is what a family was made of.

She smiled as she recalled the five children singing "Waltzing Matilda." Lucy and Gianna had to have taught the others the song. Listening to them sing this song was what Elizabeth had needed to put her mind at ease. Her girls remembered Arlo. They remembered home. They wouldn't lose touch with their Australian heritage if they moved to the United States. They were carrying it inside them. It was a part of them and always would be. Not only that, they were sharing their heritage with their friends.

Elizabeth's eyes filled with tears as she realized that they had found a new home in Montana with Jake and his kids. This wasn't the outcome she'd expected when she'd decided to visit America, but it was the best one ever. Tears of relief streamed down her face. She wiped them away, but more took their place. Her emotions were too strong. She had no way to control her feelings or to stop her tears.

Jake walked up to her. When he saw her tears, he paused, and his smile faded. He stooped in front of her chair and took her hands into his. She read the concern in his eyes. Wasn't that just like him? She'd pushed him aside, yet here he was, worried about her. If that wasn't love, she didn't know what was.

"What's wrong?" he asked.

Her emotions were getting the better of her, and all she could do was shake her head. She took a deep breath in an attempt to get a hold of herself but was unsuccessful.

"You don't have to say it." Jake's voice brimmed with sorrow and disappointment. "You've made up your mind to leave town. Hearing that Australian song made you miss home."

She shook her head. The song had affected her, but not in the way he thought.

"Then you're officially breaking up with me for good?" His tone was even sadder and filled with heartbreak.

Finally she was able to speak. "Wrong again."

"Then what?" His voice was quiet, but she heard the fear and desperation there.

She couldn't bear the pain he was feeling. She cupped his face. "I love you, Jake. And I love your kids. I don't want to live another day without any of you."

He blinked. "What?"

"You heard me. I love you."

"I love you too." Their eyes met. His were intense. Filled with strong emotion that made her heart leap. "I love you so much. I'll live wherever you want. As long as we're together."

"I've decided. The girls and I are staying in Bronco."

"Really?"

"Yes." She glanced over at the kids. They were sitting at a long table, nibbling on cookies and sipping red punch from clear plastic cups. "Our kids are already a family. I think we should make it official."

He laughed and his eyes lit up. "Are you asking me to marry you?"

She shrugged. "I wasn't, but I will if you want me to."

He grinned. "Actually my ego would prefer that I do the asking."

She smiled. "If that's the way you want it."

"It is."

She folded her hands on her lap and sat up straight. "I'm ready."

"I'm not going to do it now. Not like this." He gestured to the surroundings. The room was nice for a concert, but it was not exactly romantic.

"I hope you aren't going to make me wait too long." Now that she realized how she felt about Jake and the kids, she wanted to get the future started.

"No. I would only be hurting myself." He stood and pulled her into his arms. Then he lowered his head and kissed her deeply.

Tingles shimmied down her spine, and she kissed him back with all the love in her heart. He deepened the kiss, and she allowed herself to be swept away before she reluctantly pulled back. "We don't want to stir up more gossip."

"Speak for yourself," he said then pressed a kiss on her lips, lingering for a moment before breaking contact and leaving her longing for more.

Laughing, she pulled away from his arms, creating a slight distance between us. "Stop. People in town already believe we're engaged or soon will be."

"Really?" He raised his eyebrows.

"Yes. Apparently gossip about us is running rampant. I'm told that's normal in small towns."

He laughed. "I don't think there's any more gossip here than any other place."

"I beg to differ. No one gossiped about me on the rodeo tour." He opened his mouth to argue, and she pressed her fingers against his lips, preventing further discussion. "I would prefer that we avoid being the topic of more gossip in the future."

"So would I." He looked over at the children at the table. "We should tell the kids first anyway. You know, so they can get used to the idea of being a family."

She nodded. "Okay. But let's not tell anyone else until it's official."

"I like the idea of this being our secret for a while longer."

"In that case, I guess we should wait until we're at home to tell them. I don't know about Molly, Pete, and Ben, but Gianna and Lucy haven't learned the art of whispering yet."

Jake laughed. "I wouldn't expect any of them to be able to keep quiet when we tell them the news."

"In that case, let's go home."

Jake caressed her cheek, and she leaned into his hand. "Home. I like the way that sounds."

So did she.

Two weeks later...

"How many scoops of ice cream do you want?" Jake asked. They had brought the children for ice cream at Cubby's for a treat after a hot day filled with fun activities.

"I would love three," Elizabeth said with a grin. "That way I won't have to choose between my favorite flavors. But the sensible part of me that wants to model self-control will have to be content with rocky road and butter pecan. Sadly, chocolate chip will have to wait for another day."

Although this wasn't her first time getting ice cream here, Elizabeth was still delighted by the shocking bubblegum-pink paint on the building.

"Very mature of you," Jake said.

"I know. I'm proud of myself."

"If you want, I'll get a pint of chocolate chip to go."

She folded her hands in front of her chest and batted her eyes. "You're my hero."

"That's what I plan on being from this day on."

Elizabeth looked around. "Where are the kids? I thought for sure they would be shouting their orders at us."

"Wait here."

"What do you mean? We have to find them before they get into some sort of mischief."

Jake kissed her briefly. "I have everything under control. Just take a seat at the booth in the front and wait for us. I'll be right back."

Shaking her head, Elizabeth did as Jake had directed.

These past couple of weeks had been wonderful. As expected, the kids had been delighted when she and Jake had announced that Elizabeth and the girls were staying in Bronco and that they would all be a family soon. Ben had immediately hugged her and told her he was glad to have a mother like all the other kids at school. Pete had asked if he could call her *Mom* instead of *Mum*. Molly and the twins had asked if they could be in the wedding even though technically Jake and Elizabeth weren't engaged. It had been loud and chaotic, and she had loved every second of it.

In a moment, Jake was back with the kids. They were walking with their hands behind their backs and grinning from ear to ear. They ran and sat in the booth next to the one where Elizabeth was sitting.

"I have something to ask you," Jake said. His smile was

broad, but Elizabeth noticed a bit of nerves. He inhaled and cleared his voice. "But first, I want to tell you how much you mean to me. There was a time, not too long ago, when I believed my chance at love had come and gone. I didn't think I would ever be able to love a woman with my whole heart. Needless to say, I was wrong. You mean the world to me."

He approached her booth and took her hands into his. His were trembling as much as hers were. "I couldn't pull this off on my own, so I have five helpers."

He nodded at the kids who stood beside him, grins on their faces. Molly pulled a handwritten sign from behind her back. The word *Will* was written there. Then Pete held a sign with *You* on it. Ben's sign read *Marry* and Gianna's sign read *Us*. Finally Lucy held up a sign with a question mark written on it.

Elizabeth clasped her hands to her chest. Though she'd known Jake had intended to propose to her, she hadn't expected anything this sweet. But then, the children were a big part of their lives, and it was only right that they be part of the proposal.

Jake knelt in front of her and held out a small, velvet box. He opened it to reveal a princess cut solitaire.

"Well?" Ben said. "Are you going to marry us?"

Elizabeth smiled. "Yes. Yes, I am going to marry all of you."

Smiling, Jake slid the ring on Elizabeth's finger. Then he kissed her gently. The kids swarmed them and wrapped them in a group hug. A family hug.

It had taken a while, and for a time Elizabeth hadn't believed it was possible. She had found love again. All seven of them would live happily ever after.

* * * * *

Look for the next installment in the new continuity
Montana Mavericks: The Anniversary Gift

A Lullaby for the Maverick
by Melissa Senate
on sale July 2024,
wherever Harlequin books
and ebooks are sold.

And don't miss

Sweet-Talkin' Maverick
by Christy Jeffries

Maverick's Secret Daughter
by USA TODAY bestselling
author Catherine Mann

The Maverick's Marriage Deal
by Kaylie Newell

The Maverick's Thirty-Day Marriage
by Rochelle Alers

and
Starting Over with the Maverick
by Kathy Douglass

Available now!